Handersen Publishing, LLC
Lincoln, Nebraska

THE QUIET MAN BOOK #1

INAUDIBLE

Library of Congress Cataloging-in-Publication Data

Names: Hansen, Tevin. author.
Title: Inaudible / Tevin Hansen.
Description: Lincoln, Nebraska : Handersen Publishing, LLC, [2022] |
    Series: The quiet man ; 1 | Audience: Ages 9-12. | Audience:
    Grades 4-6. | Summary: "When a cherished sketchbook is thrown
    into the sewer, Mizzy Agnor goes on an art rescue mission, where
    she must board an Imagination Train, stand up to a hideous creature
    known as The Grundt, and escape the horrors of the underground
    before her own imagination becomes corrupted"-- Provided by
    publisher.
Identifiers: LCCN 2022026968 (print) | LCCN 2022026969 (ebook) |
    ISBN 9781647030780 (hardback) | ISBN 9781647030797
    (paperback) | ISBN 9781647030803 (ebook)
Subjects: CYAC: Imagination--Fiction. | Drawing--Fiction. | Rats--
    Fiction. | Deaf--Fiction. | People with disabilities--Fiction. |
    Brothers and sisters--Fiction. | LCGFT: Novels.
Classification: LCC PZ7.1.H36433 In 2022 (print) | LCC
    PZ7.1.H36433 (ebook) | DDC [Fic]--dc23
LC record available at https://lccn.loc.gov/2022026968
LC ebook record available at https://lccn.loc.gov/2022026969

Publisher Website: www.HandersenPublishing.com
Publisher Email: editors@HandersenPublishing.com
Author Website: www.TevinHansen.com
Artist Website: CareyGoddardDesign.com

THE QUIET MAN
1

INAUDIBLE

TEVIN HANSEN

Handersen Publishing, LLC
Lincoln, Nebraska

CHAPTER 1

Mizzy Agnor stood at her bedroom window with a look of shocked horror on her face. She'd spent all day drawing and listening to music in her room, enjoying one of the last few days of summer vacation. Standing up to stretch her legs and peek outside on this blistering hot August afternoon, she looked down below to see her older brother committing a truly horrendous act in broad daylight.

Vandalism of art.

"What are you doing?" Miz yelled at him from the open window. She had to crank up her BTE (behind-the-ear) devices because she had, once again, forgotten to charge them. She was used to always keeping spare batteries around with her, so these new rechargeable hearing aids would take some getting used to.

"I *said*...I'm getting rid of this old junk," said her brother Evan, who heartlessly tossed another of his sketchbooks into the recycle bin. "I can't believe I used to waste so much time on this junk."

When Miz heard the *click* of his bedroom door close a moment later, she stealthily crept downstairs and slipped outside to collect them, rescuing hundreds of drawings from being recycled into a telephone directory, or building insulation, or kitty litter.

"Miz, honey?"

"You okay?"

The constant *beep-beep-beep* let her know that the batteries in her hearing aids were about to die.

"I'm fine!" Miz hollered to her parents as she hurried back upstairs to secretly stash the discarded art collection where it would never be found. The last thing she needed on her last weekend with her brother was to have him be angry with her for an unauthorized art rescue mission.

With the last remaining proof that her brother used to have an imagination hidden at the bottom of her socks and underwear drawer, she padded barefoot across the hall to see if he was even remotely suspicious.

Miz thumped her fist on the door with the GO AWAY, Please sign. Instead of the sound of her brother talking on his cell with his other imagination-less friends, she was pleasantly surprised to hear a voice on the other side say, "Come in!"

Miz stood in the open doorway, perplexed. Her college-bound brother was laying on his bed, fully dressed, wearing his new school hoodie. He was staring vacantly at the blank walls with a weird grin on his face.

"Now what are you doing?" Miz couldn't help but notice how empty his room was. Her brother's room used to be filled with art. A place where she used to have her own wall, and where her older brother used to proudly hang up her art creations. Those same walls were now bare. Empty. Void of anything remotely artsy-fartsy.

"Oh, you know, just looking around," Evan said wistfully. "Hangin' out in my old room, wondering if I'm going to miss this old place."

Old room? Old place? Miz shook her head. Her brother didn't leave for college for another three days, and here he was talking about home in the past tense.

"Want to draw with me?" Miz asked, swatting her messy brown hair away from her eyes. "We could do the back-and-forth art challenge?"

Her brother was leaving on Monday, so this would be his last weekend at home. Her heart gave a painful tug to think that she wouldn't see him again until Christmas holidays or Thanksgiving break at the earliest. She'd already made up her mind that her brother would be so "grown up" by that point that he would want even less to do with her.

Turns out she didn't have to wait even *that* long.

"Nah. Too busy," Evan said, clearly not busy at all. He checked his phone, hoping for a text to save him. "Gotta get ready, you know."

Tears welled up in her eyes. Miz couldn't believe she actually thought he might say *yes* this time. That today might somehow be different.

It wasn't.

Sensing that his younger sister was on the verge of crying, Evan sat up and moved to the edge of the bed.

"Look, Mizzy…" Evan paused to think about what he could possibly say to his artistic younger sister, who had been taught by a great teacher—*him*. "I know you like art—*er*, love it. Whatever. It's just—" He sighed.

"Just what?" Miz could already feel the lump in her throat threatening to choke her.

Evan shrugged. "Art is…kiddie stuff."

Miz forced herself to look away. There were so many things she wanted to say to him. How she would miss him. How much she looked up to him. And how it felt like their family didn't matter anymore. That *she* didn't matter anymore.

"Besides—" Evan offered his best smile. "I have to pack. I'm leaving for college in a few days."

"Yeah, I know," Miz said flatly. "It's the only thing you and Mom and Dad have been talking about for weeks."

Ding!

A text message arrived to save him.

"Just a sec, okay? I have to answer this…" Evan tapped his phone screen, which of course led to him reading through an entire thread of texts while his brokenhearted sister stood in his doorway.

Miz quietly shut the door and went downstairs to see if her parents would side with her. They were both smart people, so maybe they could help her restore her brother's love of art and being creative.

"Evan won't draw with me," Miz announced as soon as she entered the kitchen. She waited patiently for their response, but both her parents were busy working at the kitchen table. Her parents enjoyed their work so much that they usually brought it home with them.

"Mom? Dad?" Miz snapped her finger, not sure if she cared that she was being rude. "Hello? I *said*…"

Mom sighed. "He needs to pack, Miz. Just give him a little space, okay? He's leaving on Monday."

Her father chimed in with, "Off to college!" as he clicked SEND on another work email.

Bzzt.

The doorbell rang, saving them.

"Doorbell!" her father announced.

Mom said, "Get that, will you, Miz?"

Miz stomped all the way to the front door, feeling foolish for acting so childish, but unable to stop it. She couldn't understand what had happened to them. To *all* of them. Her whole family. It wasn't just her brother's creativity that had shriveled up and died. To her, it seemed like she was stuck living in a house where *everyone* had lost their minds—or at least their imaginations.

When Miz opened the door—

"OOOOH!" a voice cried out.

A sketch of a grotesque man wearing a dirty hat and torn jacket suddenly thrust itself right in her face. Lifeless eyes, mouth sewn shut, a curved needle in one hand, and a spool of thick black thread in the other.

"Hey, Fenn."

Miz and the neighbor boy, Fenn Toffler, had been best friends since either of them could remember. Somewhere around was a photo album full of pictures of them hanging out in their diapers, splashing in a kiddie pool in the backyard, and early birthday parties they were both too young to remember. There were even multiple stories of them running away together when they were little.

"What do you think?" Fenn asked, adjusting his new multi-colored glasses. He was wearing his favorite superhero t-shirt for the third day in a row. "I think I'll call him…" He leaned in to whisper, "The quiet man."

Miz took the drawing. "It's really good. And creepy."

"Thanks," Fenn said. "I came up with him this morning. The quiet man drains all the creative juices from your body and leaves you a mutated mess of humanity."

His face suddenly turned thoughtful. "Kind of like most grownups, you know? Here we are on a nice Friday afternoon, sun and everything, and my parents are zoned out in front of their laptops. Yours?"

Miz handed back the drawing as Fenn stood on his tiptoes so he could peek over his best friend's shoulder and into the house, where he could see Mr. and Mrs. Agnor with their eyes locked on a computer screen.

"Yep," Fenn said, nodding. "Yours too. Wanna come to my house? We can finish cartooning up my bedroom wall. Or have a paint war in my backyard."

Miz shook her head. "Nah."

Fenn gasped. He couldn't have been more stunned if the real quiet man suddenly reached out with his long, spindly, creative juice-sucking fingers and grabbed his shirt.

"You? Not make art? Wow, this is the weirdest Friday afternoon *ever*. Maybe I'm on the wrong planet, and Queen Miz woke up in a really bad mood today."

Miz tried to soften the scowl on her face. Her best friend looked worried that she might punch him.

"You okay?" Fenn asked.

Miz huffed. "I'm fine," she said, then stormed past him without bothering to shut the front door. Her best friend—a boy, but who at least had an imagination— gently closed the door and hurried to catch up.

Fenn easily found her across the street. "Um, Miz?

You're sitting in Mr. Drittsekk's yard. Are you actually trying to get us murdered? That guy loves his precious yard more than life itself. He hates kids—especially us."

Miz sighed. "I'm on the curb."

Fenn sat down beside her, but kept peering nervously over his shoulder as if Mr. Drittsekk—a skinny, bearded, overall-wearing retiree—would come tearing around the corner wielding a steel rake over his head, screaming at them to *stay away from the trees!* A thick row of cypress trees blocked the view of the house, so maybe they were safe.

Miz thought it was a bit odd to see this strip of grass so long today. Mr. Drittsekk hated kids, *passionately*, but adored his yard. The grass stood a few inches higher than normal, so it was easily tall enough to hide the rusty steel cover.

A manhole.

If she wasn't in such a bad mood, Miz might have noticed the cover had slid off. Just a bit. Enough to reveal a sliver of dark around the edge, like a thin black crescent moon.

Men in orange vests sometimes went down inside, to fix things that needed fixing, pulling off the heavy lid with a special tool, but always putting it back.

"I've got a bunch more," Fenn said to break the long silence. "Wanna see them?" He held out his sketchbook filled with all his fantastic, creepy creations.

Miz glanced down at the sketches, always curious about other people's art, and what their imaginations came up with. She wanted to say something nice, to compliment his artistic talents. She wanted to tell him that if he kept it up, he really would be a game designer one day.

She *wanted* to, but didn't. Mostly because she was too busy glaring across the street at her house, where her imagination-less family were staring at screens—or walls.

"You always show me these characters you create for video games," Miz told him. "You can't even code!"

Fenn looked hurt. "You don't need to code to be a game designer. You have to know basic scripting and stuff like that. But I'm going to be a character artist. I'll dream up all the heroes and villains. Just like this sewer dweller I came up with last night."

He handed over the drawing.

A rat.

A *huge* rat with a messy mop of curly hair stared up at her from the page. The evil-looking rodent with the bright pink eyes was as big as a sixth grader, with claws like a velociraptor, and filthy sharp teeth twisted up into a wicked grin.

Miz was about to compliment him on the detail of the drawing when two figures suddenly appeared out of nowhere, blocking the late afternoon sun.

Two girls.

13

"Hey, Reiny." Miz didn't need to look up to know who it was. She could smell who it was standing there.

Reiny Greene, her ex-best friend, placed her hands on her hips. "It's Reianna," she said. "Not Reiny. Not anymore."

Miz pretended to suddenly be very interested in the rat drawing. "I like your new perfume, *Reianna*. Smells like salt and vinegar potato chips. Or maybe—" She sniffed. "No, definitely sour cream and onion."

Fenn snorted.

The other girl standing there sucked in her breath, as if no one should dare to speak to them like that.

"What did she say?" the girl snapped, then repeated herself in a snippy voice. "What did *she* say?"

Tracey Tispe.

Miz and Fenn knew her too—or at least knew *about* her. Same age, same grade, but from a different school. Soon they'd all be going to the same middle school. Tracey was the one teaching her ex-best friend that it was more important to be *cool* than to be *kind*.

Quick as a snake, Tracey reached out and snatched the sketchbook right out of Fenn's hands. "That looks like a stupid drawing of a rat," she snorted. "A filthy, disgusting rat." She tossed it back, sending a dozen sketches scattering over the grass.

"It is a rat," Fenn said, busy replacing all the loose pages back into his sketchbook. "It just doesn't have a

14

name yet. Maybe I'll call it Tra—"

Miz elbowed him.

Fenn rubbed his side. "Never mind."

The two girls placed their hands on their hips in such a perfectly timed way that it nearly caused Miz and Fenn to burst out laughing. Clearly these two had picked up their new personalities from a reality TV show or some social media influencer.

"We're going over to Mike Tulette's house," Reianna said, fishing for a reaction. "His parents go out every Friday night. He's having a party."

"Mm-hm. Sounds great," Miz said, bored.

Tracey Tispe whipped her hair around, expertly. "We were *invited*," she said, as if they should be jealous of such an honor.

Fenn made a disgusted noise. "That clown knocked me off my bike a few days ago," he told the two dressed up girls, both wearing skirts and too much makeup. "I think Mikey forgot that he and I used to hang out in our diapers together—you know, doing baby stuff, making mud pies, taking naps, and lots of breastfeeding."

The two girls snorted in disgust. "Ugh."

Miz kicked his foot. "Have fun at your party," she said to the girls, still not meeting their eyes. "Bye." She kept staring at the picture of the rat. Even in the fading sunshine, it made her skin crawl. Could a rat get that big?

"Come on, Reianna. Let's get out of here," Tracey said, pulling her new bestie away. "We shouldn't waste any more time hanging out with these…" She glared down at them like they belonged in the sewer with the rats.

Miz finally looked up. "Losers?" she suggested. "Art nerds?"

"Drawing dorks?" said Fenn. "Palette posers?"

"Gouache geeks?" Miz added.

In a huff, the two girls left.

At least a dozen cars drove by before either of them said a word. Miz felt like she was done talking for the day. But her one remaining best friend still had the motivation to be creative.

"So?" Fenn said.

"So what?" Miz had a stick in her hand. A fallen branch from one of Mr. Drittsekk's perfectly groomed trees. For the last ten minutes, she'd been smacking it on the road, hating mean people, and ignoring her good friend.

"Well, if I like art," Fenn said, "and *you* like art…"

Miz threw the stick. "I don't care about art. It's kiddie stuff! Don't you understand that? We're all going to grow up and get boring jobs and live ordinary lives anyway, so who cares?"

Fenn's shoulders slumped, even though he knew she didn't mean it. He also knew that when she got like this, it was best to leave her alone for a while. He picked up his sketchbook and turned toward home.

"You *do* care, " Fenn said as he walked away.

The rat sketch was left behind.

"Hey! You forgot your—" Miz waved the sketch in the air, but it was too late. Fenn was gone. It didn't matter, since he only lived a few houses down. She would see him tomorrow.

More cars drove past.

Miz sat on the curb for so long that her butt went numb. Eventually she lifted herself up off the curb and dragged her feet toward home. She was still carrying her friend's artwork, though she refused to look down at the picture of the ugly rat with curly hair.

Chit-chit-chit.

Down inside the foul-smelling sewer just a few yards away, at the bottom of a rusty metal ladder…

Something *moved*.

An immensely large sewer dweller with four powerful incisors, stained a sickly yellow, and so gruesomely long that even the men in orange vests would run away…had been listening. The chattering noise, faint but unsettling, was the sound of its grinding teeth.

CHAPTER 2

Miz dreamed she was being stalked throughout her old school. It wasn't even a dark and stormy night. There was no full moon, no howling wind, and no screeching animals in the distance. This was a regular sunny school day with lessons, tired teachers, bells, pop quizzes, and obnoxious in-class behavior.

A cruel boy with a round face and a mop of curly hair kept throwing things at her. Pen cap. Chewed gum. Wads of crumpled paper—whatever was handy. Every time it happened, she would turn around and yell at him to stop. But the mean boy's face wasn't right. He appeared human from the neck down, but with the face of a sewer dweller. Huge eyes, long whiskers, and chattering teeth.

A giant rat.

If she had to make a stop at her locker, he was waiting for her. Hitting, biting, scratching, and making her life miserable at every turn. These attacks were carefully planned, always taking place when no one else was around. No one except the rat bully's group of rat friends, who would all stand around and watch, wearing a stupid rat grin on their ugly rat faces.

When she found herself cornered outside of the school, the huge rat bully came at her from out of nowhere, ready to fight. Ready to claw her eyes out.

Down came the first blow.

Slash.

A sharp claw made its way into her soft skin.

Slice.

A warm, sticky trail of red traveled down the length of her arm. Then the rat-faced boy opened his mouth, showing off four long incisors, discolored and ground to a sharp point. When those ugly brown teeth came slowly toward her, mouth opening wide, wider, widest, about to sample her face…

Chit-chit.

Chit-chit.

She woke up.

"Holy crapola." Miz sat up in bed, breathing hard and covered in sweat. She looked around her bedroom, unsure of where she was at first. A sunbeam peeked through the curtain from where she didn't quite close it all the way.

Just a dream, Miz thought. A very realistic, rat-infested dream that (hopefully) would be forgotten by lunchtime.

Glowing numbers from her wall clock revealed the time in bright orange.

"Eight-thirty already?" Miz groaned for the loss of early morning art she could have accomplished. She'd slept more than an hour past her normal wake up time.

Reaching for her BTEs, she immediately cursed under her breath, mad at herself for forgetting to place her hearing aids on the charger before falling asleep last night.

"Big deal." Miz shrugged it off as she strapped on her hearing devices. "The charge should last until dinnertime… maybe."

Still dressed in yesterday's clothes—white shorts and purple tank top—Miz went across the hallway and knocked on her brother's door.

"Come in!"

Permitted entry, Miz opened the door and found her brother wide awake and playing a video game on his flat screen TV. The same TV her parents had offered to put in her room just as soon as her brother left for college, even though she hadn't asked for it.

"Hey, Miz. What's up?" Evan said, eyes focused on the screen. He was concentrating heavily on his newest *shoot-*

em-up, *blow-em-up*, *kill-em-all* video game.

Miz watched for a minute, fascinated by the artwork behind the game. Her brother was one of those people who insisted that video game designers were special people born with a rare gift. Not artists and writers, who work hard to create the environments, characters, and storylines that he and all the other gamers of the world loved so much.

A mug of dirt-flavored water sat on his nightstand, right next to his college class schedule. She'd peeked at it before and saw that nearly every class started with the word "business."

Business Management
Business Law
Business Ethics
Business Administration
Business *blah, blah, blah.*

"You drink coffee now?" Miz pointed to the steaming cup of java next to his alarm clock.

"Sure," Evan said. "I'm old enough. Besides, everybody at college drinks coffee, you know that."

Boom, boom, boom.

Blast, blast, blast.

"No, I didn't know that," Miz said. "Why would I know

what people at college drink? Probably alcohol, which is very bad for you. Over thirty percent of college students go there to party."

"What?!" Evan chuckled. "How would you know a thing like that? You're too young for grownup stuff."

"I heard Mom and Dad talking the other day."

Her brother played on.

The graphics were mesmerizing. But the game's storyline had way too many guns, explosions, and burning cars for this early in the morning.

"Want to do something with me?" Miz asked. "We don't have to draw or make art. We can go ride bikes or walk down to the park." She swallowed hard. "Like we used to."

Those words again.

Used to.

Evan kept playing. "Sorry, kid. I can't."

Kid? Miz shook her head. "Why not?"

Her brother suddenly yelled at his character on the screen. "Come on, I hit that guy!" Soon he was so involved in a car chase through the streets of a very realistic downtown that he forgot somebody was standing there.

"Hm? Oh. Sorry, Miz. Not today," her brother said. "I'm waiting on a phone call. It's important." His eyes never left the screen.

Click, click, click.

Shoot, shoot, shoot.

When Miz couldn't stand it anymore, she scooped up his brand-new burgundy college hoodie from the floor and threw it right in his face.

"Hey!" Evan shouted angrily, as if his little sister had just insulted his college of choice. Just not angry enough to do anything about it, or stop playing his video game. He batted the sweater away while never letting go of his controller.

Click, click, click.

Bang, bang, bang.

"What happened to you, Evan?" Miz glared across the room at him. "You used to be fun. You used to do things with me all the time. Now all you do is…*that*." She flicked one hand at the TV, which she would tell her parents she did *not* want in her bedroom after her older brother left for college on Monday.

Miz asked, "Where'd your happiness go?"

"My…*what*?" Evan looked surprised by such a strange question. "My happiness?" He laughed it off. "Hey, I'm feelin' pretty happy right now. This is my last weekend at home, then I'm off to college. I just want to chill out and look at stuff. Maybe later this afternoon we can—*Yes*!" He cheered after completing the level. Another level began right away, so he never finished what he was going to say.

Miz had never *truly* yelled at her brother in her whole

life. The hot, bubbling, spit-flinging kind of anger surging through her body right now, making her throat hurt and her cheeks burn, was about to change all that.

"Look at stuff?!" Miz shouted. "Instead of spending time with me, or doing something with your family, who you're not going to see for weeks and months, you'd rather…*look at stuff?*"

Evan yawned. "Miz, come on. I don't want to ride bikes or walk anywhere. And I don't want to draw goofy pictures. Art is *your* thing, not mine. I quit drawing a long time ago. Besides, I can't—"

Ding!

A text message arrived. He answered it promptly, then received a quick answer, so had to reply again, and again, and again.

Tap-tap-tap.

This time, Miz didn't bother to gently shut her brother's bedroom door. She closed it with so much force that the noise reverberated through the whole house. She'd never really slammed a door in her life, either. Not hard enough to shake the walls.

From downstairs came, "No slamming doors!"

Miz dragged her feet downstairs and into the kitchen, where she found her parents in the exact same positions as the day before. Different clothes, different coffee mugs, same scenario.

"Hi," Miz said. "Happy Saturday."

"Morning," her mother said, offering a quick side-hug. She was studying a home decor website, carefully scrolling through pictures of candlestick holders and throw pillows.

"Sleep okay?" her father asked with only the top of his head visible over the laptop screen.

Miz told the truth. "Nope. I had a bad dream about getting attacked at school by a huge rat. A rat bully."

"Rats?" Dad peeked over his screen, alarmed.

"Yeah, this guy." Miz showed her parents the detailed drawing of the biggest, creepiest, most bouffant-haired rat ever to roam the sewers.

"Mm," her mother said. "Very chichi."

Miz studied the drawing from arm's length. "It's one of Fenn's best ever, I think." She would give it back to him this morning—after she apologized for yesterday afternoon when she'd acted so *un*-chichi.

"Don't worry, sweetie," her father said as he sent out another work email on a beautiful Saturday morning. "We don't have any rats in this area."

Miz wasn't so sure. "Doesn't every city have rats? Rats live where people live, don't they?"

Click, click, click.

Type, type, type.

Miz poured herself a bowl of Cocoa Krispies and ate her breakfast in silence. The cereal's famous *snap, crackle, pop* wasn't as loud this morning, but only because her hearing aids were barely charged.

"What are you two doing today?" Miz asked, rinsing her bowl and placing it in the dishwasher. "It's a nice day outside."

Her mother said, "Ah, is it?"

"Work," her father replied.

Miz kept her cool and tried again. "Maybe we could all go for a bike ride," she suggested. "Like we used to."

Again, there it was—*used to.*

Her father looked up, confused. "Bike ride?" His face grew thoughtful, as if suddenly recalling all the bike rides they used to go on as a family.

"Sure, sweetie. Just not right now," her father said, though offered no further details about possible times, such as *later, after lunch,* or *maybe this afternoon.* Just more superbly crafted emails to his co-workers.

Click, click, click.

Type, type, type.

Miz left the house and wandered over to the curb outside Mr. Drittsekk's house. The cranky old man with the overalls and scraggly white beard wasn't out mowing today, so she was safe for now. She sat and waited for Fenn, who was still at home, probably eating breakfast while hunched over a drawing at the kitchen table. He was the only person she knew who loved art more than she did.

He would be out soon, ready to hang out, and yesterday's argument already forgotten.

She waited a long time, but no Fenn.

Instead, two girls came walking up the hill, talking loudly and fake-laughing as they approached.

"Hey, Reiny—uh, Reianna," Miz said. "Hey, Tracey." Forcing herself to be nice, she said, "What are you guys up to today?"

"*Guys?*" Tracey Tispe looked supremely annoyed. Her face seemed incapable of anything but sneering. "We're not *guys*, Little Miss Hard-of-hearing. We're—" She paused, unable to think of a suitable alternative.

Miz tried to politely keep her mouth shut. But the lingering anger and frustration from dealing with her family led to the poor decision of mouthing off to a girl like Tracey Tispe.

"Hey, it's okay. I get it," Miz said. "Sometimes a girl like you needs a little extra time for a thought to filter through."

Reiny snorted, while Tracey Tispe appeared confused, as if unsure whether or not she'd just been insulted. When it finally clicked that she *had* been insulted, her face broke into a snarl, ready to retaliate.

"At least I can hear properly," Tracey Tispe said with a smirk. "No problem there."

Miz didn't flinch. "I can hear just fine, thanks.

Sometimes I just choose not to listen to people when they say something really dumb to a person with a disability."

Tracey Tispe balled up her fists.

"We're going to Mike Tulette's house," said Reiny, attempting to defuse the situation. She'd also secretly took her ex-best friend's advice and skipped the sour cream and onion perfume today.

"Yeah, *again*." Tracey Tispe leaned over and stuck her face out. "Reianna and Michael are—" She sniffed. "Well, someone like *you* wouldn't understand, but they're—" She couldn't finish because she was giggling too hard, making little pawing motions on her new BFF's arm.

Reiny's cheeks glowed red.

Miz had never seen her friend get embarrassed. Not even when Mike Tulette pulled too hard on her shirt in PE class during a co-ed soccer game a few months ago, accidentally ripping the sleeve and exposing her training bra for all the boys to see.

"You're going out with *him*?" Miz said, stunned. "Like…actual dating? The same boy who ripped your shirt in PE? The same boy who shoved Fenn off his bike? The same boy who got in trouble for peeing on the school walls last year? Him?"

Reianna flipped her long blonde hair. "We're not dating. Nobody says *dating* anymore. Geez, wake up. We're going together—I guess."

Miz suddenly felt like her breakfast may come back up after hearing this news. Until just a couple of months ago, Miz and Reiny were inseparable. Always drawing, painting, or crafting for endless hours. Now that they were a few days away from starting middle school, everything had changed. Had her ex-best friend's love of art shriveled up and died too?

"*Ugh*," Tracey groaned, a revolted look on her face. "Is that the same stupid picture from yesterday? A disgusting rat?"

Miz proudly showed it off. "I can make you a copy if you want. My parents have a really good scanner," she said, unable to stop the train wreck of words that came pouring out of her mouth. "Then you can tape it to your bedroom mirror while you put on all that gross makeup you're wearing. I'll make you a copy too, *Reianna*. Then you can hang it on your wall, right next to your picture of Mike Tulette."

Her ex-best friend, still undeniably kind despite her recent efforts to fit in with the cool crowd, merely sighed and shook her head. She looked disappointed in her old friend.

Tracey Tispe had zero kindness. She reached out and grabbed the sketch before Miz could even react.

"Hey! Give that back!" Miz shouted, forcing herself to remain seated. Rising up off the curb would be a clear sign of aggression. And there was no telling how far a girl like Tracey Tispe would take things. Bullies don't take breaks. Not even during the last few days of summer vacation.

"Rats belong in the sewer," Tracey said as she shoved past Miz, purposely knocking her over. She stood on Mr. Drittsekk's grass, hips posed just right, and dangled the drawing over a large black hole. "Dare me?"

The manhole was wide open.

A cast-iron cover that weighed 250 pounds had somehow turned up missing. There were no men in orange vests working today, but the heavy lid was gone. Or had it been stolen? Miz had heard about this: people stealing manhole covers and selling them for scrap metal.

"Um, Tracey?" Miz stood up, but kept her distance. "I know you hate my guts, but I'm warning you—be careful."

"Yeah, Tracey," said Reianna. "Get away from there. You don't want to fall in. There could be...*things* down there. Gross things."

"Oh? You mean like rats?" Tracey laughed, then let go of the drawing with a malicious, "Oops."

"NO!"

The sketch of the giant rat with curly hair was dropped down into the hole, swallowed up by the darkness.

The two girls left, laughing and complimenting one another on their collaborative nastiness.

Miz stood at the edge of the dark hole, peering down

into the depths, debating about what to do next. Should she go get Fenn? Her brother? Should she have her mom call Reianna's mom and demand an explanation about why her daughter had suddenly turned into such a little (*bleep*).

Miz let out a deflated sigh. "Middle school is going to be so much fun," she said quietly. "Especially with those two."

Just like when she had to dig through the recycle bin to save her brother's art-filled sketchbooks, her best friend's art was also in need of rescue.

And she was going in after it.

CHAPTER
3

Playing flashlight hide-and-seek used to be a big thing at their house. Miz and her brother used to play for hours, turning off all the lights, hiding under beds, behind the shower curtain, or trying to keep still underneath a pile of clothes.

Used to.

Nothing but misty memories and vague visions of days long gone, full of shadows that no light can penetrate. No more games of hide-and-seek in the dark—or even a flashlight.

"Don't we have a flashlight in this house?" Miz hollered from the kitchen. "We used to have a million of them. Now we have a ton of batteries, but no flashlight."

Her parents hadn't moved from their spots at the kitchen table, except to refill their mugs of dirt-flavored water. Neither one flinched as their only daughter dug noisily through several kitchen drawers, huffing loudly, trying to locate some artificial light before setting off on her art rescue mission.

"Try the downstairs office," her father said. "The small drawer next to the computer."

Miz rummaged through several more drawers in the shared office before giving up. "Which computer? The iMac or the PC?"

Her mother worked from two separate computers, while her father worked mostly on the laptop or the iPad.

"Try both," her mother said as she clicked through pages of novelty picture frames that might add some much-needed pizzazz to the living room.

"Yes!" Miz quietly cheered to herself when she discovered a flashlight in the drawer next to the fancy new printer. Beside her mother's Xmas gift—a top-of-the-line LaserJet printer—was the watercolor canvas Miz had painted for her months ago. It still hadn't been hung on the wall, as promised.

"Got it! Thanks."

"Mm-hm," her mother said.

"Bye, sweetie," said her father. "Stay out of trouble!"

Flashlight in hand, Miz left the house while revving up

the handheld dynamo light. Navy blue, with a see-through body full of gears, springs, and other moving parts. It was the kind of flashlight you had to keep squeezing, otherwise the light would go out.

Zuzz-zuzz-zuzz.

Miz stood over the manhole, shining the wimpy beam of light down into the opening. A gaping black hole big enough to swallow up light, art, and young girls.

"Stupid, useless thing." Miz stuffed the flashlight into the pocket of her favorite white denim shorts, which were about to be ruined.

The grass tickled her thighs when she sat down.

"Should've worn pants for this expedition," Miz muttered. "And rubber boots. And a face shield. And nose plugs." She debated on whether she should postpone the mission until she was better prepared.

Or better yet, go get help, Miz thought. Then again, her bare legs were already dangling into the hole, daring whatever *thing* was down there to reach up and grab her foot.

Nothing reached up to grab her.

Miz climbed down the ladder, each time feeling around with one foot before placing her full weight on the next lower step.

When her eyes were at street level, about to disappear from view, she felt a twinge on her left leg. A shiver shot up her back, turning her entire body rigid. Both hands clenched tight to the rung she was holding. Her legs had suddenly locked up, leaving her incapable of simply climbing back up the ladder.

"Uh-uh-uh…" Miz let out a pitiful moan, unable to utter a single word to fend off the underground attacker. Was it one of the men in orange vests? The workers who waved to them sometimes? Or was it something hideous?

She didn't dare look down. It was too easy to imagine a slimy, grotesque hand as it slithered up her leg, groped around her waist, and further…

Just like at school the week following the training bra incident, when she watched Mike Tulette sneak up behind Reiny and shove his hand right into her front pocket, leaving behind a folded up note. A secret note, like all the other boys and girls seemed to be more interested in— instead of making art, having fun, and being kids.

"*Foo-ahh.*" Miz exhaled when she realized what happened. No decayed hand was touching her. It was only her imagination, filled with too many late-night images.

Clink.

Clank.

Clunk.

The windup flashlight slipped from her pocket. That was the funny tingling sensation she'd felt on her leg. Clanging and banging off several rungs on the way down, the flashlight hit the bottom, then bounced somewhere out of sight.

"Just lovely," Miz said, which was something her mother would say when anything went wrong.

With more of her body inside the tunnel than out, Miz decided this was the best way to stand up to the girl who had heartlessly tossed her friend's artwork into the sewer.

Strictly by feel, *tap-tap-tap* with her left foot, followed by the right, she made it to the bottom without slipping, or falling off the ladder. Better yet, without the ladder collapsing in a heap, leaving her unable to climb back up.

"*Pfft*. It's not so bad down here," Miz said after she'd jumped off the last step and landed on her feet. "I thought I'd be scared out of my mind."

This was, by far, the bravest thing she'd ever done. She wasn't sure if she was more surprised by how calm she felt while standing at the bottom of a huge, dark tunnel, or the fact that it was so quiet.

A trail of murky water ran in both directions, and the sloped brick walls were covered in brown sludge. But the small area at the bottom of the ladder was perfectly dry.

Like a great flashlight in the sky, the sun shone down on her through the hole. One step in either direction meant she'd be swallowed up by a darkness so thick that it might wrap around her small frame, then drag her away.

Standing next to the ladder, she was still inside the

small circle of weak sunlight.

So was her friend's sketch.

"Fenn, you are *luuucky*," Miz said, amazed that her friend's artwork had somehow missed landing in the filthy water. All she had to do was grab the sketch, climb back up the ladder, and be done. The missing flashlight would stay missing—a sacrifice to save her friend's artwork.

It happened so fast.

A noise came out of the darkness.

Chit-chit-chit-chit!

"Who's there?" Miz found her voice, but the rest of her body wasn't cooperating. Her brain had locked up, leaving her an easy target for whatever was lurking down here in the dark.

Somewhere in the tunnel, teeth chattered. Not the tiny chatter of a small rodent, but something much larger.

And *close*, too.

Her heightened senses could easily detect the creature's heavy footsteps in the foul water. Even on low power, her hearing aids could pick up the sound of its sharp claws dragging along the hard cement, getting closer with each *click-clack, click-clack*.

Whatever it was, the underground stalker had to be no more than a few yards away from where she stood with her eyes wide, legs trembling, and senses on overload. Though it still hadn't stepped out of the darkness to attack, she could feel its eyes watching her from the privacy of its underground home.

"Leave me alone!" Miz screamed.

When her brain finally unlocked, she was about to quickly bend down, grab the sketch, then scurry up the ladder.

When she reached out her hand—

Click.

A large forefoot with long, dirty claws stomped on the sketch. The four sharp claws were attached to four grotesquely long pinkish toes, which led up to a muscular, hairy arm.

Beyond that was a wide black nose, twitching and sniffing, making its thick, wiry whiskers move.

Two pink eyes, each as big as her fist, watched from the shadows. And just above the mean, narrow eyes was a mess of curly hair, matted and covered in filth.

A colossal rat.

The rat bully from her dream was standing only a few feet away. The same vivid dream that her subconscious mind had created from the fear brought on by staring too long at her friend's sketch…was *real*. Had the dream been a premonition? A warning?

"Please," Miz whispered softly. "Don't hurt me."

She wanted to scream at the sewer dweller to leave her alone. But intense fear of what might happen if she stood up for herself had choked off her usually strong voice.

She could hear its ragged breathing. She could see the awful mouth, full of stained teeth. She could sense that it was enjoying this. Terrifying her so badly that she thought she might lose control of her bladder.

Chit-chit-chit!

With such a delightful terrorizing of the young girl coming about with hardly any effort, the giant rat removed its clawed foot from the drawing, leaving behind a muddy footprint—a claw print—right in the center.

The giant rat skulked away, teeth chattering.

Or was it…*laughing?*

Miz seemed to remember reading somewhere that rats have the ability to laugh, though the sound is too difficult for humans to hear without using special equipment.

The sound of the giant rat's voice bounced off the walls, echoing through the tunnel. Thankfully, the noise grew quieter as the sewer dweller wandered off in search of another easy target.

Miz stood there, breathing hard and shaking all over. Her panicked mind couldn't seem to figure out if what had just happened…had *really* happened.

Was that really the rat bully from her dream? Did the men in orange vests know about this? Did Fenn know too? How had he come up with the idea to draw an enormous rat with a mop of curly hair?

A million questions filtered through her mind as a small voice cut through the dark, startling her.

"*Phew.* That was close," the voice said.

Miz looked down at her feet, where a much smaller (but equally filthy) sewer dweller crept out of the shadows.

A small rat.

This much more friendly-looking rat gazed up at her with two solid black eyes, then opened its mouth to say...

"Miz."

CHAPTER
4

In the pages of every book, graphic novel, or short story Miz had ever read, rats were made out to be the bad guys. Ugly, awful, sinister creatures that bite, scratch, carry disease, and make girls scream. Just the mere sight of rats can cause depression, or chronic sadness. In movies and TV, rats were always depicted with glaring red eyes, filled with malice and hatred.

This rat's eyes were a bit sad.

Even with its wretched appearance—mangled whiskers, patches of fur missing, and a thick, scabby tail dragging limply behind—this small rodent looked harmless. The complete opposite of the monstrous sewer dweller that had just crossed her path.

"Did you just say…*Miz?*"

"Yes," said the rat. "That's your name, isn't it? I heard you up there yesterday, talking to your boyfriend—the one with the sketchpad. I heard you again this morning, speaking with those two girls."

Miz needed a moment to collect her thoughts. She was, after all, conversing with a rat, and *not* hallucinating.

"Fenn's not my boyfriend," she finally replied. "He's just a boy who happens to be my friend."

The rat stared vacantly up at her, unmoved.

"Do you have a name?" Miz asked, feeling a bit foolish for even asking.

The rat sniffed. "My name is Rattus," it said. "My full name is Rattus Norvegicus. But to most of you above-grounders, I'm just a sewer rat."

Miz felt her heartbeat slowly returning to normal. Her breathing was more relaxed, though the smell attacking her nostrils was still sickening.

"My real name is Mizabella," she told the rat. "But hardly anybody calls me that. My dad wanted to name me Marlene, but my mom liked the name Isabella, so they…" Her words trailed off because of the way the rat was looking at her, sly and uninterested.

"Combined them?" Rattus suggested. "Yes, you humans are so very clever." He clicked his teeth.

Miz felt slightly insulted. As she'd gotten older, she'd

noticed how the few creative kids she knew spoke softly, while the least artistic people always spoke with a sharp tongue.

Rattus was a bit of both. "So what exactly are you doing down here? This isn't the kind of place for such a clean girl with hair that smells like fruit, and—*mmmm*—such tasty skin."

Miz stiffened, making a raspy noise in her throat.

"I mean to say…" Rattus stood up on his back legs. "Today is a nice day. At least *up there*, it is." His head bobbed up and down, nosing up toward the circle of light near the top of the ladder. "Shouldn't you be playing with other kids your age? Enjoying the sunshine instead of lurking down here with the rats?"

Chit-chit-chit.

In the dark, she could hear more of them. Other rats, with their tiny feet scurrying through the tunnel. Sometimes a fragment of light would reflect off their tiny black eyes as they watched from the shadows.

"I, uh…" Miz cleared her throat. She was still having a hard time dealing with the fact that she was speaking with a rodent. "I came down here to get something. *That*, actually."

"This?" Rattus said. "I peed. Sorry."

A small piddle was right in the center of her friend's artwork, which was now ruined—or at least at the point where Miz no longer wanted to pick it up.

"Rats pee everywhere so we can advertise our availability," Rattus said, then wiggled his whiskers in a way she didn't understand.

Miz gave a confused look. "Availability?"

Rattus picked at a scab on his neck. "You're a girl, right? So you like boys, right?" His black eyes sparkled in the dim light. "Or perhaps other girls? That's okay too. Some girl rats prefer other girls, and some boy rats prefer other boy rats."

"I like *art*," Miz said defiantly.

"Me? I like food," Rattus said, oblivious to the girl's agitation. Then his black eyes bulged out. "Are you carrying? Did you bring anything down here with you? Some raw meat? A bit of rotten fish perhaps?" He licked his bleeding lips.

Miz patted her pockets. "Sorry, I only have a flashlight." She looked around but saw no sign of it. "I *had* a flashlight. It's gone now."

Rattus tilted his small, furry head. "It's here somewhere, I promise. Your flashlight is just hiding in the dark someplace. Just like *him*. That great big sewer dweller that wandered through here a moment ago."

Miz shivered at the thought. "What was that thing anyway? It was huge! I thought it was going to—" She couldn't bring herself to utter the words *eat me*.

"The Grundt," said the rat, then trembled. "At least

that's how he's known to many down here."

Miz nodded as if she understood, but clearly didn't. "But what *is* it? How did a rat get that big?"

Rattus scratched himself inappropriately while he pondered the question. "From what I've heard," he finally said, "the Grundt used to be the very active imagination of a young boy. A boy that loved to draw and paint and write excellent poetry. A boy without a mother. A boy who lived with a drunk and disorderly father that, shall we say… knocked all that creativity out of him."

"Oh." Miz felt a lump in her throat. She recalled an incident in fourth grade, when a boy she hardly knew came to school one day with a terrible black eye, but no story to tell. Other curious kids asked questions. *Was it a slapshot to the face? Was it an animal attack?* But all they received was a vacant stare in response. And the next week he was gone, never to be seen at school again. Even their teacher looked sad when a few students raised their hands to ask about what happened to the quiet boy who got hurt.

"What do you mean, *used to* be an imagination?" Miz loved her creative nature, but she'd never once thought about it like a real, tangible thing.

"Exactly what I said," Rattus told her. "Every person is born with an imagination. But when boys and girls begin to grow up, or when they stop using their imagination so much, or not at all…"

"They come here? To the sewer?" Miz looked around at her surroundings. With its constant *drip-drip-drip* of brown water, an aura of decay, and the putrid smell, this was perhaps the only place for an unused imagination to linger. To wander around aimlessly in the dark tunnels, searching for a bit of light.

"Perfect setting, don't you think?" Rattus commented.

Nothing could have prepared her for what her new furry companion said next.

"This—" Rattus spread his thin, scabby arms out wide. "—is where imaginations come to die."

CHAPTER 5

When Miz placed her feet on the middle rung of the ladder, it became clear that something was terribly wrong.

The rusty bolts came loose.

"AHH!" She had to jump out of the way as the entire structure broke free of the wall, then came down with a tremendous crash of broken metal.

"Told you it would fall over," Rattus said when the girl who'd climbed down the ladder had tried to climb back *up* the same way. "Rats may do a lot of bad things, but we don't lie." He sniffed. "Okay, we don't *always* lie."

Too heavy to lift, Miz's stubborn nature had her at least *try* to do the impossible. This was another bad idea.

When Miz attempted to lift the heavy ladder back into

place so she could climb out, the only result was slicing open her finger. A jagged piece of rusty metal easily tore through her delicate skin.

"My finger is bleeding," Miz said, examining the cut on her index finger. The gash was short but deep.

"Is it?" Rattus looked pleased. "May I?"

"May you what?" Miz said sharply, pulling her hand away. "Don't you dare come near me."

Rattus looked ashamed. "How rude of me," he said. "We've only just met, and here I am asking for a drink of your—" He paused, then scratched at the mites that infested his filthy fur. "This way! Follow me."

The rat walked away.

Miz followed the sound of tiny claws on the wet cement, and listened to the voice of a rat who could see just fine in the dark.

A few dozen steps down the smelly, slippery tunnel, walking in complete darkness with her hands out in front, feeling the occasional spiderweb on her face, stepping through unimaginable filth, feeling eyes watching her closely, sensing a threat around every corner, choking back the urge to scream…

A dot of light appeared.

Miz focused on the tiny dot of yellowish-gray light, feeling braver as she watched it grow slightly larger with each step. She imagined herself inside an enormous flashlight, making her way down the long tube, all the way to the tip, where the light shined out.

Crunch.

Imagining she was stuck inside a giant flashlight was better than thinking about the raw sewage that kept splashing up onto her bare legs, or the cringy jolt that shot up her back after the underfoot *crunch* of another dead insect.

"Make sure to keep up," Rattus warned. "If the other rats see that you're with me, you might be safe. If you were alone down here, this far into the maze…"

Miz quickened her pace. Unable to help it when her thoughts turned as black as her surroundings, she wondered if this could be a trick. A trap? What if this small rat wasn't leading her toward the exit? What if he was taking her to the giant rat? The Grundt. Or was he bringing her to a feast with hundreds of other starved rats, whose thousands of tiny, sharp teeth would soon enjoy a tasty meal? *Fiesta de la Joven*, which her decent understanding of Spanish meant *Feast of the Young Lady*.

Rattus suddenly stopped. "I'm not trying to trick you," he said, "if that's what you're thinking."

Miz's breath caught in her throat. "Are you telling me that you can—?" She'd learned from her science teacher at school that rats were smart. But she never dreamed they were *this* smart. "You can read my mind?"

Tsst! Tsst! Tsst!

Hsst! Hsst! Hsst!

The rat was laughing.

"No, I can't read your mind," Rattus said. "And I don't think I'd want to, either. Reading the mind of a girl your age sounds dreadful. And depressing." He traveled on, leading the visitor farther away.

"I just didn't want you to think I was taking you straight to *him*," Rattus continued. "A rat so strong that he can chew through brick and bone. Even us rats are smart enough to stay far away from that one."

Miz cringed. "I thought it was going to attack me back there." She wished she could block the awful image from her memory—a rat so big it would haunt her dreams for years to come. "I've never been so scared in my whole life. I couldn't move."

Rattus stopped again. "I think—?" His whiskers twitched. "I think that particularly large sewer dweller was once an imagination even more active than yours, if you can believe it. An imagination that could have gone on to do great things. Helpful things. What's more, I believe the boy the imagination once belonged to also attended the same middle school that you start next week."

"My new school?" Miz walked beside her tiny travel companion, sometimes straining to hear what he was saying. She wanted to stay as close to him as possible, but without stepping on his crooked tail. "How do you know I'm starting middle school next week?"

Rattus' black eyes reflected a bit of light. "Like I told you before…I hear you talking up there. We *all* hear. Rats have excellent hearing, and we are excellent at hide-and-seek. You people make far too much noise. We hear you through the walls, from the darkest corner of the garage, or while we're rummaging through the kitchen cupboards after you go to bed."

Miz didn't fully understand, but kept quiet and listened attentively as they traveled farther down the tunnel, headed toward the dim light at the far end. If she didn't pay close attention to the drone of the rat's voice, her imagination might wander off, leading her to overthink, or dream up all sorts of scary things hiding in the dark.

Other rats were listening to their conversation as they passed. So many tiny eyes, lurking in the dark.

"At that middle school of yours, where I've enjoyed many meals in the trash bins…" Rattus gave a sharp little squeak at the thought of such excellent finds, and could momentarily think of nothing but delicious rotten food.

Miz knew he must be talking about the large blue bins outside the middle school library. A place she'd already visited a few times over the summer, but urged him to go on.

"The Grundt, whom you had the displeasure of

meeting earlier, was once a very talented football player," Rattus went on. "Bigger and stronger than most boys his age. He was quite good at winning games, and brought to the school a series of championships. All that praise and adulation carried on into high school, winning game after game, taking home trophy after trophy. But instead of attention from friends and faculty, the boy's heart craved something more."

"What?" Miz asked, though she could guess which path the story would take. She'd read lots of books where the school's most popular boy—usually the star quarterback— was dating the most popular girl at school.

"Let me guess…" Miz rattled off a few book titles with the same old clichéd storyline. "He fell in love with the prettiest girl in the entire school. I'll bet she was head of the cheerleaders, right?"

Rattus shook his head once, then twice, and let out a sneeze so bad it made his eyes bleed—red tears.

"As you already know, some girls who are exceptionally pretty are only marginally smart," Rattus said in his clever way. "And some marginally pretty girls are exceptionally smart."

Off the top of her head, Miz could already picture a girl like that. Reiny, her ex-best friend, who was in all the accelerated classes (with her and Fenn) had suddenly begun to change, critiquing her own body, and claiming she wasn't pretty. Things they'd never worried about—or had even *considered*—until the beginning of summer vacation, when everything went wrong with their friendship.

"The Grundt was homely," Rattus went on. "As homely as this tunnel is long. Not much in the way of a personality, either. On top of his thick, empty skull was a mess of curly red hair that most girls would die for—or is it kill for? Either way, you know how girls can be when it comes to their appearance, always worrying about what others think."

Miz could name a few people like that. Girls her age that were suddenly so worried about their clothes, makeup, and what other people thought of them that it changed them. Especially a girl like Tracey Tispe, who dressed and acted a lot older than she was, with so much of her self-esteem reliant on what others thought and said about her—especially boys.

Rattus gave a dismissive wave. "Whatever the expression," he said, "all those girls who hung around the football games loved to stroke his hair, yet couldn't get past the fact that although he was quite popular, and exceptionally good at throwing a football, he was also quite boring to be around. He was excruciatingly dull."

Clack-click went the rat's claws.

Squish-splat went Miz's filthy shoes.

Runners that were once white, but were now splattered

with black and brown, continued in a straight path down the filthy tube. A never-ending maze of dark tunnels.

"Then what?" Miz asked.

"While all the other boys on the football team chased after the prettiest girls," Rattus went on, "the Grundt set his mind on a smart, bookish girl who was far off the radar of every boy in school. A sweet girl, freckled and spectacled, with a mess of curly red hair—just like his. Only this girl was not interested in football, or going to parties—or *him*. She was interested in someone else."

"Who?" Miz guessed it had to be another popular boy. "Probably the captain of some other team, right? Lacrosse, or soccer, or something like that?"

Rattus shook his head. "Nothing like that at all," he said, smacking his scabby tail on the wet cement. "This girl had a great hunger in her heart for an artsy-fartsy boy. A quiet boy, who was much smaller, kinder, and gentler than the football hero. The boy she craved affection from had personality in good supply, able to make her laugh in class, make her feel good inside, and make her fall in…fall…"

Bloop.

Rattus relieved himself.

"Fall in love?" Miz asked, stepping back from the small pile of dark, shiny pellets next to her foot.

"Yes, *that*." Rattus took a moment to get a hold of himself, mouth-breathing from nearly having to say that word to finish the story. "Rats do appreciate companionship, but we don't…we can't…"

Miz nodded. "I get it," she said. "Rats don't love each other. Just please don't get sick on me." She wanted to say please don't *die* on me. "You're my only way out of here. Are you sure you're okay?"

Rattus took a few shaky steps. "Don't worry, I'm not going to die on you," he said. "I still have a little time left. A few days at least, or maybe a few weeks. Rats don't live much longer than a couple of years, and I'm nearly two and a half years old."

Arms swinging at her sides, Miz realized that she was no longer holding her hand up to her nose, so either the smell wasn't so bad this far into the tunnel, or she was simply used to it by now.

Soon her rat friend was steady enough on his feet to keep moving. The light at the end of the tunnel was getting larger. Big enough to walk through, even though it was impossible to tell what was on the other side. Whatever was out there had to be better than a filthy sewer, with hundreds of tiny black eyes watching her.

They walked in silence. The only sounds were their feet splashing through the trickle of nasty water.

"So the Grundt—uh, the football star," Miz corrected herself, "fell in love with the smart and kind of pretty girl, but she didn't love him back? And that's it?"

Rattus glared up at her as they walked. "No, that isn't it at all," he replied. "It's never that easy. Since the artsy-fartsy boy didn't know this girl had feelings for him, he went about his days much like you."

"Me?"

"Drawing, painting, and creating," Rattus told her. "Using his imagination constantly, until the day he—" *Chit-chit-chit* went his teeth. "Gave up."

Miz recoiled. "Gave up? You mean he—" She'd heard rumors about a boy from another school that ended his life over a girl he loved, but who didn't love him back. Was it true? She didn't know because the rumor came from Tracey Tispe, the type of girl who would make up such a story.

"Nothing like that," Rattus told her. "The boy was not suicidal. I simply meant that he gave up on a lot of things. His passion. His drawing. His painting. His artwork. The boy who once dreamed of becoming an artist, gave it all up one day. He simply quit."

"Why?" Miz tried to reason why a talented artist could just stop one day. To her, quitting art was unthinkable.

"Turns out the freckly smart girl was severely lacking in common sense," Rattus explained. "She wrote the boy a long and detailed letter—*very* detailed. The real problem started when the Grundt got a hold of that letter, when he carried her books for her while walking to class, trying to show the curly-haired girl what a sweet big boy he could be. But the foolish freckled girl handed over the book with the letter still inside. Reading those words crushed his already hardened heart. It tore him apart."

"A love letter?" Miz had read many stories like that, but they always ended happily. This one didn't sound like one of those fairy tales.

"All the Grundt's anger, all his rage, all the abuse he'd suffered from his own father was taken out on this poor boy," Rattus said, then paused to nibble his flaky skin. "The attacks were always carefully planned out. Taking place when no one else was around. The Grundt would appear from the shadows, hiding underneath staircases, waiting around a blind corner, forever catching the victim off guard. And always surrounded by a crowd of his football friends, who would take delight in seeing this young boy being tormented."

Miz felt awful for the boy who'd suffered daily at the hands of some football star twice his size. If she'd known him, maybe she could have helped to stop it.

Or would she?

Would she have the courage to stand up to someone so much bigger? Tracey Tispe had a mean streak as long as the tunnel, but she was a good three inches shorter than Miz, with skinny arms and bony legs sticking out from the short skirts she always wore. And still, Miz's stomach would cramp up whenever there was a confrontation.

She felt like crying when she discovered the answer was...*no*. The opportunity to stand up to someone—or some*thing*—much bigger and stronger (with the added fright of long, sharp, disease-carrying claws and elongated teeth that could easily bite through her leather running shoes) had presented itself earlier.

When the Grundt had come shuffling along, her entire body seized up, leaving her completely helpless. It made her feel utterly useless to not be able to stand up for herself. To be brave when it was time to be brave. Instead, her lack of courage had made her feel empty. Worthless.

"Look!" Rattus flicked his nose toward the large circle of light. "We made it!"

Miz felt a sense of relief wash over her as they approached the end of the tunnel. Although brighter, the light was still a hazy color, gray and dull. A large opening big enough to walk through greeted her. But even with her excellent eyesight, it was still hard to tell what was beyond the mist.

"What's out there?" Miz could make out rough shapes, though it was impossible to tell if they were trees, low-lying hills, or piles of dead things. Was something out there moving around? More rats?

Miz took a deep breath, then stepped into the light. Right into the welcoming hands of whatever was on the other side.

Crunch.

Her skin turned icy cold when hundreds, or thousands, or possibly *tens* of thousands of insects, dead and alive, crunched underfoot.

"What the—? Oh." Miz sighed in relief when it turned out to be only rocks and gravel she was stepping on, not a sea of dead bugs. The lack of visibility filled her with a sense of dread, as if the gray mist was hiding something.

"Ahh!" Miz yelped in pain when her toes smashed into a long, unforgiving piece of metal.

Tracks.

"A train will be along shortly," Rattus said, then scratched his itchy fur mites until it arrived.

CHAPTER
6

A heavy fog outside the tunnel made it impossible to tell what was out there. Cold and miserable, Miz stood there in nothing but shorts and a tank top while she watched the mist swirl around her ankles. It was so dense that she could hardly make out her brightly colored runners, or even locate her new rat friend.

"Pick me up!" Rattus demanded, circling somewhere down at her feet. "Quickly, before you lose me. Then you'll never find your way back."

Miz had never held a sewer rat before. And it wasn't something she wished to experience now.

"I, uh…"

Rattus gave an impatient squeak. "I promise not to

pee in your hand," he said. "I already went. Just now. So I won't have to go again for at least a few minutes."

To take her mind off the fact that she was now holding a fairly large sewer rat, who was constantly biting and gnawing at his itchy skin, she bothered him for more details from the story as they awaited the mysterious train.

"Didn't the teachers help?" Miz asked, already shaking from the cold. "Or his friends? Why didn't anybody help him?"

"Who?" Rattus said. "The artsy-fartsy boy?"

"Yeah, him." Miz had read enough books to know that every story had elements of good mixed in with all the bad stuff. Standing in the fog with her teeth chattering, holding a rat that—from tip to tail—was nearly as long as her arm, awaiting some kind of ghostly train to arrive, she decided that right now would be an excellent time to hear some *good* news. A bit of light amid the gray.

"What about his family?" Miz asked. "Couldn't he tell his parents he was being harassed at school? I'll bet they could have done something. Maybe tell the principal, or the police, or somebody who could help."

Rattus wrapped his tail around her wrist. "The boy told no one about the attacks," he said. "Not the teachers, not his parents, or even his sister."

A sickly noise cut through the air.

Ooooooo.

The train's horn sounded like it was in desperate need of repair. A low, ghostly moan that could be close, or possibly miles away. The constant *tick-tick-tick-tick* of wheels chuffing along the tracks grew steadily louder.

"Ah, the train." Rattus heard the sound of wheels grinding on the steel tracks long before the girl, whose hand he was trying not to pee in. "Our ride will be here shortly," he told her. "Then we can see about finding a way out."

Miz felt more confident upon hearing this news. She'd never been on a train before, so couldn't help but hope it would be a train like the Hogwarts Express, a classic steam locomotive.

Ooooooo.

Before the train arrived, there was just enough time to finish the story of the artistic boy versus the football star.

"What about the girl in the story?" Miz had to use both hands to support her rat friend, since the little ball of fur was heavier than he looked.

"The curly-haired girl, you mean? The girl who was stupid enough to leave her suggestive letter inside the pages of her text book, where that oversized football goon could steal it?"

Miz glared down at him. "That's not fair," she told the rat. "That girl wasn't stupid. She was just—well, she didn't know what she wanted, I guess."

"Mm-hm." Rattus plopped down onto his backside, hunched over like he was about to make another mess.

"Hey! You said you wouldn't!" Miz wanted to drop the rat, but relaxed when he informed her that he wasn't peeing, but simply had a terrible itch that required immediate scratching.

"These darn fur mites," Rattus said, clawing away.

"Just hurry up," Miz said. "It's gross."

Scritch-scratch.

"The girl, I think she——" Rattus nibbled himself again. "Yes, I believe she changed her mind about the artsy-fartsy boy. One day she simply chose someone else. An older boy from a different school. Captain of the lacrosse team, I heard. Or was he captain of the soccer team?" He sniffed. "I can't recall every detail."

Miz felt a pain in her heart. She couldn't believe the girl from the story would do such a thing. She wanted to believe the rat was making it up as he went along. But apparently *rats don't lie*. Or at least it seemed this one didn't.

"The girl just changed her mind?" Miz asked, stunned. "She fell in love, then fell out of love? Just like that?"

Rattus glared up at her with his two round, glassy black eyes. "Just—like—that," he said, then let out a satisfied squeak when the itch was relieved for now.

Settling back against her palm, Rattus tilted his head back to speak. "When the curly-haired girl found out about all the bullying nastiness, and those unprovoked attacks, and that *she* was the cause of it…" He ground his teeth.

"What'd she do? She just ignored it all?" Miz asked in disbelief. "Acted like it never happened?" She was starting to like this girl less and less as the story went on.

Rattus nodded. "She dropped them both and went on to the next best thing. Last I heard, she was about to head off to college to become a school counselor. Funny how life works out sometimes, isn't it?"

Miz dropped her gaze. "Yeah. Funny."

Whump…whump…whump.

The train took forever to stop rolling. Miz wondered if it would ever stop. Had the brakes failed? The awful, high-pitched grinding noise coming from the tracks was so loud that Miz desperately wished to cover her hearing aids to block out the sound. She couldn't because she was holding on to a sewer rat.

Mouth-breathing because of the infection in his lungs, Rattus said in a wistful voice, "I once had a girlfriend."

Miz waited for him to go on, since he seemed hesitant to say anything more about his lady rat.

"We were together a long time," Rattus finally said. "Over a month. That's a long time for a rat. We even tried to leave the sewer, deciding to run off and start a new life together. But soon we ran out of food, and then she…"

The rat trembled in her hand. Whatever had happened,

the memory still clearly bothered him.

"Never mind," Rattus snapped. "I just wish this decrepit old train would stop. Then we can leave this fog behind. I wonder if the train has a dining car?"

Miz could tell he didn't want to talk about what happened to him and his girlfriend, so changed the subject. "So that's the end of the story? The Grundt, the boy, and the smart girl lived happily ever after? Just far, far away from each other?"

Rattus made the same noise again, an ultrasonic *squeak-squeak* that resembled laughter.

"No, no, no," he said, annoyed. "This is no fairy tale. These things didn't happen a hundred years ago, or fifty years ago, or even twenty years ago." He coughed and wheezed. "My older-older-older brothers and sisters were still alive when all that stuff was going on. That's how I know the story. And how I know" —he wiggled his crooked whiskers— "all about those lovely trash bins down at the middle school."

Chuff, chuff, chuff.

Finally, the train came to a full stop. A dull gray passenger train with dents and dings, cracked windows, and the smell of smoke coming from the engine appeared out of the mist. The narrow door automatically opened with a horrible *creeeeeak*, inviting them to board the neglected train.

65

An empty train.

A passenger train with no passengers.

Miz sighed deeply. "It's no Hogwarts Express," she said, "but it's better than nothing." After more squeaking and wriggling in her hand, she carefully placed her rat friend on the bottom step of the train, then watched him climb up.

"Are you coming?" Rattus said.

"Yeah, I'm just...thinking." Miz looked around one last time, debating on whether or not she should go back the way she came. Behind her was the grimy, foul-smelling sewer. In front of her was a rundown train that looked like it may fall right off the tracks. She was about to turn around and walk back to the sewer, alone, when her new rat friend poked his head around the corner.

"By the way..." Rattus clicked his long teeth. "Did I mention that the Grundt knew your brother? They went to school together."

Standing at the bottom step, Miz felt the blood drain from her face, as if the gray mist had just slithered up her body and wrapped itself around her heart.

Her brother was the artsy-fartsy boy.

CHAPTER 7

Climbing up the steps and getting that first view of a classy train will often cause the boarding passengers to gasp in awe at the beauty and elegance. Rows of comfortable chairs, large windows to watch the passing scenery, and the smell of wonderful foods cooking in the dining car.

Miz gasped for a different reason. More of a cough than a gasp because so much smoke was billowing from the old train that she could hardly take a full breath without choking on the fumes.

Deciding it was probably wise to board the train rather than be left standing in the mist, alone, Miz climbed up the four creaky steps and stood on the platform. When she got her first view of the inside of the train, she was able to sum up the experience in just a single word.

"Ugh."

"Yes, very accommodating, isn't it?" Rattus looked pleased. "I've heard the noise of this train many times before, though I've never had a reason to climb aboard. I wasn't even certain it was a real train, since I rarely leave the sewer."

Rattus led the way down the aisle, along the heavily worn carpet that ran the length of the train. Dark yellow and light brown—two colors that Miz hoped were simply the chosen colors of the carpet and not because the train had been used as a public toilet. Which was exactly how it smelled, even with her shirt pulled up, breathing through her tank top.

"I wouldn't dare use *that*, however," Rattus said as they passed a closet-sized bathroom covered almost exclusively with mold—dotted and black. "The bathroom appears to have contracted a bad case of *stachybotrys*, the kind of mold that will make you violently ill if breathed in too long."

All the wooden drawers had been kicked in, laying in scattered piles, most with tiny teeth marks. There were lots of words and phrases scribbled on the wall. Most were too faded to make out, but Miz thought one might say:

Welcome to the rat race

Miz took one look at the foul bathroom and had to hurry away. "Yeah, I think I'll just hold it, thanks—forever. There's no telling what diseases I'd get in there. And besides, the toilet is clogged. And it has no seat."

Rattus sniffed. "Actually, one of those cell phones you humans are so fond of are much dirtier than a toilet," he said. "Maybe not *that* toilet, but you get the picture."

Miz cringed, thankful she didn't have to go too badly. "Can we talk about something else, please?" She was going to ask about departure times when the train suddenly shook so violently that it knocked her off balance.

"Hurry up! Sit down!" Rattus scurried underneath the nearest table that *wasn't* broken, where he leapt from the floor to the seat, then up onto the table, so he could peer out the cracked window.

Phoof.

"Aw, this is gross." Miz sat down and kicked up so much dust that she held her breath as long as she could before taking another. "I'm glad I don't have really bad allergies like my older brother, otherwise I'd be coughing my lungs out right about now." She looked to her new rat friend for a response, but he had grown quiet. His black eyes stared intently out the dirty window.

"See anything?" Miz gently placed her forehead on the cracked glass. Outside was nothing but fog and shadows. Fearing what may be hiding *in* those shadows had her turning away from the window. Peering around the inside of the train was just as creepy, if not more so.

It all looked the same.

Two cars in either direction was about as far as she could see, until the vestibule blocked the view. The cars she could see all looked the same. Deteriorated so badly that it was hard to picture what the train may have once looked like. Most of the windows were cracked and dirty. Every single table was either broken, tipped over, or both. The few curtains that hadn't fallen off their rods were cut and torn, or hanging by a few threads. And no matter where she moved, a metal spring would poke through the seat cushion and dig painfully into her backside.

Ooooooo.

The train whistle moaned again. An awful, discordant noise like an entire orchestra blasting a different note, alarmingly loud and hopelessly out of tune.

"Who's driving the train?" Miz asked. What if others were aboard? Others like the scary villains and beasts that Fenn was always drawing, often explaining (in great detail) how they attacked, what weapons they used, and what happened to the victim's body after they were…

Killed.

Miz shivered, pushing away the morbid thought.

"No one," Rattus answered sharply, then went back to staring out the window.

Something was up with her rat friend, but Miz kept quiet and let him work it out. She wanted to ask him how long the ride would be. How far were they going? How would they get back? Then she remembered that he already told her that he'd never ridden the train, only heard it from the sewer.

"You okay?" Miz asked after a long, silent ride. The train had picked up enough speed that the bumping and jostling lessened as they sped down the tracks, traveling in one of four possible directions. Or was the train going in a fifth direction...*down*?

Rattus quietly said, "She ate my toes."

Miz thought she'd heard wrong. "Ate your—what? Who?" She studied the rat's furry body, her eyes settling on his left foot. The one with a couple of toes missing, causing him to walk with a noticeable limp.

Rattus wheezed before going on. "My ex-girlfriend," he finally said. "Not long after we ran away together, searching for a new place to live, we ran out of food. We became so incredibly lost that we couldn't even find our way back to the sewer..."

Miz listened and did not interrupt. She even flashed her best fake smile to help him feel better, despite the story of nibbled digits making her stomach turn.

"I woke up one morning and found she'd already eaten her breakfast," Rattus went on. He cradled his left foot, wiggling the three remaining toes. "I slept through the first one. The second one, I was just starting to come around after a long, miserable night. Then, I woke up."

Ooooooo.

The train whistle moaned again.

Rattus let out a soft whimper. With watery black eyes, he looked up and said, "Thank you. I've never mentioned that story to anyone before. I feel better for having told someone."

"Sure," Miz said. "No problem."

Without another word, the rat with eight fingers and eight remaining toes, jumped from the table to the seat, then from the seat to the floor. He'd detected the scent of rotten food somewhere on the train.

"Hey! Where are you going?" Miz gripped the table so hard that her knuckles turned white, mostly because she didn't want to be left alone on the Nowhere Train.

"To see if there's anything to eat!" Rattus said before scampering away to the next box car.

"What do I do?" Miz hollered. "Just sit here?"

The last thing she heard her rat friend say was, "Use your imagination!"

After narrowly escaping an attack by the Grundt, then walking through a filthy sewer, and now riding a spooky train with nothing but fog visible from the windows, she found it very difficult to use her imagination.

With a new school year just days away, her thoughts were mainly concerned with survival. Especially after losing her best friend at the beginning of what was supposed to be an amazing summer. Would she always be pushed around by girls like Tracey Tispe? Would Fenn continue to be harassed by guys like Mike Tulette? Would her new life at a new school be worse than living in a sewer? Or would middle school be more like the writing on the bathroom wall—a rat race?

The very moment she pictured Stigg Middle School in her mind—

Creeeeeeak!

Thunk, thunk, thunk.

When the train squealed to a full stop, Miz stared out the window, hoping to see something familiar. The fog had cleared just enough to reveal the outline of an endless row of trees. Beyond the line of trees was a two-story structure. A building that she recognized right away because she'd been there before.

"You're kidding me," Miz said with her face pressed up to the glass. "Stigg?"

As soon as she realized that her new middle school was within walking distance, she heard the *hssss-clunk* of the door opening somewhere behind her.

The train was kicking her out.

CHAPTER 8

Miz began to wonder if she was in the middle of another dream as she slogged her way through a field of the thickest, gooiest mud. The kind of muddy clay that stuck to the soles of her shoes and made her feet grow heavier with every step.

The mist swirled around her shivering body, clinging to her bare skin, and blocking the view of whatever might be out there. In the back of her mind, she still clung to the hope that this was all simply a bad dream she could wake up from at any time.

"But if this is only a dream…"

Slurp.

"Why are my legs so tired?" Miz bent down to rescue

her left shoe from the mud, only to lose the other one on the very next step. She fished it out, tied the laces together, then hung the muddy runners around her neck.

Walking barefoot through the mud was strangely comforting. It reminded her of childhood. But what if somebody was watching from the shadows?

Seeing no one else around didn't stop her from worrying that she'd be ridiculed for doing something that other kids her age had stopped doing a long time ago.

"I wonder what Reiny and Tracey would say if they could see me now," Miz said with a snort. "They'd probably laugh their heads off, or tell the whole school I still like to play in the mud. And how I still do stupid things like—" She stopped herself before saying, "Things like draw, paint, and make art."

Checking over her shoulder was a bad idea. The heavy mist had swallowed up the view of her wretched ride, giving rise to a new fear. How could she possibly get back to the train if she couldn't see it? Following her own footsteps back would be pure guesswork. What if she wandered off in the wrong direction? Would Rattus come looking for her? Or would she continue to slog her way through endless muddy fields until she eventually collapsed from exhaustion?

"You've got this," Miz told herself. "Don't look back. Just keep going forward. Keep—going—forward."

Each step in a forward direction…

The world cleared up.

Each step in a backward direction…

The world grew darker.

Tall, pointed black spears reached high into the air, packed tightly together to form a thick wall. There was a narrow gap in the wall of trees, so that's where she headed. Determined, but still fighting back tears every dirty, mud-squelching, awkward step of the way.

"Yes!" Miz cheered. "Finally."

Just through the opening in the row of trees, the fog cleared up enough to reveal a near-perfect view of the school. Stepping out of the mud and onto solid ground was enough to produce a weak smile. The concrete walkway led straight up to the school entrance.

"Aw, sick." Miz took one look down at her mostly brown legs, and gagged. Mixed in with the sloppy brown were bits of stringy black, and squares of white. She forced herself to believe it was only mud.

After dropping her filthy shoes where the mud met the concrete, she hurried up the paved walkway, climbing several sets of stairs, and leaving a trail of muddy footprints that led right up to the school.

STIGG MIDDLE SCHOOL

At the beginning of summer vacation, before their relationship soured, Miz and Reiny (and Fenn too) had ridden their bikes all the way over to S. M. S. to survey what would soon be their new middle school. To peek through the windows, check out the basketball court, soccer field, and (though none of them said it out loud) wonder if they would remain friends.

Miz reached for the door handle.

Schools nowadays are designed with safety in mind, equipped with metal detectors, bulletproof glass, and full school lockdown the moment the nine o'clock bell rings.

The front door to Stigg Middle School opened without any resistance. Just the small *click* of the plunger retracting, followed by the sound of creaky hinges.

"Hello?" Miz took a few tentative steps inside the building, worried that she may have inadvertently set off a silent alarm.

The school was so quiet.

"Is anyone here?" Miz stopped where the foyer split off into three different hallways.

An entire section was devoted to all the accolades and achievements the school football team had accumulated over the years. Among the plaques, banners, and pennants was a large glass display case full of polished trophies.

Beside the glass display with all the trophies were three framed photographs of the football team, dressed in full uniform, posed in front of the scoreboard. Most of the team smiled, but a few had their eyes closed from blinking at the wrong time, and one or two made an intensely deranged face right when the camera had snapped the photo.

Stepping closer, Miz wasn't even aware of how heavy she was breathing. Or the fact that she was grinding her teeth. Or that her fists were clenched.

"You've got to be kidding me," Miz said in hardly a whisper. "It can't be—*him*."

In all the pictures of the football team, the same three boys were in the back row, making themselves appear big and intimidating. Two pudgy-faced boys, arms folded, with their chins up and chests puffed out, posed menacingly on either side of the boy in the center, who stood taller than the rest, wearing a smug look on his babyish face, with a mop of curly reddish-orange hair.

Below the picture was the team roster. She only had to read a few of the players' names before her breath caught in her throat, like the air had just been knocked out of her from a vicious football tackle.

Top row, center, were the names:

GRAHAM PIKK

TERRY GRUNDT

MICAH STORTAPER

Staring back at her were the same boys who had made her brother's life miserable while he attended middle school. The ones from Rattus' weird love story on the train.

With a sudden sick feeling in her stomach, Miz tore her eyes away from the picture before she became ill. Or before she did something stupid, like rip the pictures off the wall and smash them into a million pieces.

"HELLO!" Miz stood still and tried to pick up on any of the typical school sounds. Muffled voices, hurried footsteps of late students, or the sound of rustling paper from inside one of the classrooms.

What she did not expect to hear was somebody hissing at her from down the hallway.

"Psssssst!"

Some boy was waving at her. Only the upper half of his body was visible as he leaned out of the first classroom on the left. She recognized him even from a distance.

"Fenn?" Miz could hardly believe her eyes when she realized who it was beckoning her to come closer.

"Hurry up, Miz!" hollered her best friend. "Come on, before the teacher gets here!"

Miz jogged toward him, thrilled to see a friendly face. Fenn disappeared from view just seconds before she reached the doorway. A huge wave of relief calmed her anxious mind just as soon as she got her first look inside the classroom, allowing her whole body to relax.

This was *her* class.

A new classroom, larger than her old one, with wider windows and entirely different decor, but filled with the same kids from the previous school year. Some she had seen intermittently over summer vacation, and some she hadn't seen since the last day of school. And yet here they all were, welcoming her with warm smiles, excited hand waves, and asking if she'd had fun over the summer holidays.

"Hi, Miz!" said Katherine Harpiser, a bookish girl that chewed her hair so much that she once had to go to the emergency room to have a hairball removed—a story that made her semi-famous. "Did you have a good summer? You look great!"

"Oi! Miz!" shouted Aedan Krype, a good friend that moved to the USA from Namibia, and who last year tried to teach her how to properly kick a soccer ball, though he called it football. She appreciated how he didn't give up on her, even though she never did get the hang of it.

"Um, hi." Miz shyly waved back at her old classmates, feeling a bit unsettled by seeing so many familiar faces gathered in one room. She was about to politely make up an excuse to leave when one smiling face caught her attention.

Reiny Greene, her ex-best friend, pointed to the desk in front of her—the only empty seat left inside the crowded classroom.

"Hurry, Miz! I saved you a seat!" Reiny said. "Same seating arrangements as last year! Isn't this great? Middle school is going to be so much fun."

Drawn in by the buzzing excitement and nervous energy of the class, with everyone awaiting the arrival of their new sixth grade teacher on the first day of a new school year, Miz half walked and half stumbled over to her old desk. Middle row, third desk back, with Reiny seated behind, Fenn on her left, and surrounded by a sea of familiar faces—which, sadly, also included a couple of students she didn't particularly want to see.

"Yo! Miz!" Mike Tulette hollered from two rows over. His voice had changed over the summer—much deeper. "How come you're not wearing your Stigg t-shirt like everyone else? Did you forget?"

Every single student in class was wearing either a dark red or bright blue STIGG MIDDLE SCHOOL t-shirt. Emblazoned on the front was the school's mascot. But it was hard to tell if it was a bear, a large rat, or some other animal.

"I…didn't get one," Miz told him, surprised for two reasons. One, because he'd spoken to her without swearing, sneering, or making fun of her. And two, because his eyes were actually semi kind today, instead of narrow and calculating. His face showed no hint of its usual smirk.

"Oh well," Mike said. "I'm glad you're here, Miz!"

Tracey Tispe was there too, sitting on the opposite side of Fenn, who was busy scribbling a note.

"Hi, Miz!"

"Oh. Hi, Tracey." Miz found it strange to see her *not* dressed up like she was going to some boy's party. Instead of her usual skirt and crop top, she wore an oversized Stigg Middle School t-shirt, a modest pair of shorts, and no socks or shoes. The bottom half of her legs were covered in dried mud—same as Miz.

Same as everyone in class.

Miz fit right in.

Tracey Tispe leaned over to whisper, "How was your summer vacation, Miz? Mine was great. Our family spent two weeks in Chicago. We got to visit a bunch of popular places like Cloud Gate and Navy Pier—all that fun stuff. Did you know that Chicago is the most rat-infested city in the US? Totally lit, right?"

"Um, sure," Miz said. "Yeah, totally. I…guess." She took her seat. And not a moment too soon.

"Shhh, everyone!"

"There she is!"

"Ms. Galdamme is coming down the hallway!"

Seconds after she sat down, Miz felt a light tap on her shoulder. This was the same secret signal from last year. It meant that a private note was coming her way.

With the same well-rehearsed motion, Miz pretended to reach up and stretch her neck, then grabbed Reiny's note and pulled it into her lap without anyone noticing. Before she had a chance to open it up and read it, a hush came over the entire class.

A quick shadow momentarily filled the doorway, then a woman carrying a stack of papers came bustling into the room.

Their new teacher had just arrived.

CHAPTER 9

Ms. Galdamme was a slender young woman with long dark hair wrapped neatly in a bun, and held together with two fine-pointed hair sticks. The frames of her glasses were a rusty red color that matched her dark red STIGG MIDDLE SCHOOL t-shirt.

Miz liked her right away. It appeared that their new teacher genuinely wanted to be here, offering them all an extra-wide smile that made her dark eyes glint as she peered around the classroom, checking out all the new faces. Having a cheerful teacher would be quite a change, since most of the students in the room (including Miz) had been under a male teacher the last two years in a row. Although good teachers, they had rarely smiled in class because of rowdy students like Mike Tulette and his friends, who were always moving around, passing notes, belching loudly, and being a general nuisance to everyone else.

"Good morning, class!" said Ms. Galdamme after she'd finished writing her name on the whiteboard.

"G'morning, Ms. Galdamme!" said the whole class.

Miz jumped in her seat.

The chorus of voices sounded eerie and rehearsed, as if they'd done this a hundred times before. Miz gave an ill-timed greeting that had (thankfully) gone unnoticed, otherwise Tracey Tispe or Mike Tulette might poke fun at her and get the whole class laughing.

Today, though, Miz didn't think that would be the case, since everyone seemed to be in a good mood. Every student had eyes only for Ms. Galdamme.

"First off, I want to welcome you all to middle school," said Ms. Galdamme as she paced the front of the room, going back and forth in quick little steps. "I'm sure that some of you are nervous about what to expect this year, so…" She reached inside one of the drawers in her desk and pulled out something small and silver, wrapped in crinkly paper. "To break the tension, I would like to start off the new school year by doing something fun."

Thump, thump, thump!

Desks rattled on the floor. Students were buzzing in their seats, so full of excitement that they were practically bouncing up and down with anticipation.

Written next to the teacher's name on the board were two more words: *White Mystery*.

Miz guessed the teacher wanted to jump right into class expectations and school policy, or possibly discuss tough subjects like racism or some other heavy topic. She quickly found out that was not the case at all.

"Well, pups? Now that we're all here and starting to get settled in," said Ms. Galdamme, scratching at her neck, "I think it's time we get to know one another by asking a few questions."

"Like what?" asked Reiny, whose foot accidentally bumped against Miz's foot. At least Miz thought it was her friend's foot that had knocked against hers, though it felt *longer*. And the accidental smack was followed by a funny scraping sound on the floor, as if something had slithered out of the way.

"Oh, things like what you did over the summer, or when's your birthday," Ms. Galdamme replied. "Just some simple get-to-know-you questions before we get too deep into the dirty, icky parts of middle school. I'll go first, so you can learn a little bit about me, and then I'll ask a few questions about you. Sound fair?"

The whole class agreed with an enthusiastic eruption of cheers. And when the teacher revealed the prize she held in her hand, twenty-four students leaned forward in their desks, a rapturous look in their eyes at the thought of winning the sugary treat.

Airheads, the rare "mystery white" flavor.

"Can anyone tell me…" Ms. Galdamme smacked the candy against her left hand—the one with several small black tattoos that could've been shaped like little spiders. Her fingernails, painted as black as her hair, gently scratched the side of her face. "Hmm. Let's see, can anyone guess…what month I was born?"

Jillian Frekk, quiet and exceptionally smart, was the first to raise her hand. "January?" she suggested, sounding unsure of herself. "No wait—the month before January. March!"

"Correct, Jill! Good job." Ms. Galdamme beamed at her new student, then tossed her a treat.

Jillian tore off the wrapper with nimble fingers and gobbled up the treat in a few quick bites. The sugar must've entered her bloodstream quickly. She clung to the edges of her desk so hard that the metal and wood creaked and groaned under the pressure.

Mike Tulette waved his arm in the air, waiting for his turn instead of shouting the answer like he used to do.

"Ms. Galdamme?"

"Yes, Michael?"

"I guess…um, September?"

Ms. Galdamme winked. "Good job, Michael." She grabbed another silver package from the box on her desk and tossed him a prize. Again, the treat was quickly devoured, and possibly bits of the wrapper too.

Miz laughed quietly and found herself smiling at the idea of the teacher being so nice to everyone, even for getting the wrong answer. She had daydreamed this very same thing many times in the past, thinking how wonderful it would be if no kid was ever made fun of for getting a wrong answer in class.

"Let's see, can anyone tell me…" Ms. Galdamme waved around another white mystery treat, while two dozen kids tracked her every move with their greedy eyes. "Can anyone guess…where I was born?"

Twenty-four hands shot into the air, leaving only Miz with her hands in her lap. Something was clasped in her hand, held tight, kept hidden from the teacher's watchful gaze.

The note.

Seated nice and straight, eyes up to give the impression that she was paying attention, Miz carefully unfolded the small piece of paper while the other students rattled off their answers.

"Were you born in an alley?"

"Between the walls?"

"On a boat?"

While collecting their prizes and accepting the teacher's praises, Miz quickly glanced down at her lap so she could read the one word note:

Welcome

A nice gesture from Reiny, who was acting like they were friends again.

"I've got another good one for you," Ms. Galdamme said to her eager students. "How old am I?"

"Ooh, I know!" Fenn was about to jump out of his seat, he was so excited to win a prize.

"Yes, Fenn? What's your best guess?" said Ms. Galdamme. "I'm much younger than you may think."

"Two years old!" Fenn shouted.

"Correct!" said Ms. Galdamme, beaming at her student. "Good job, Fenn! Good job."

Miz noticed how their new sixth grade teacher said this a lot. *Good job*. It was the same thing her mother and father used to say to her when she was little, after accomplishing some basic task, and especially after creating some splotchy bit of art that wasn't all that good. Hearing those words—"Good job, Miz!" —used to make her feel good. Until the day it didn't make her feel good anymore. Then it made her feel ashamed, as if she hadn't done a good job at all.

Ms. Galdamme grabbed another handful of candy from her desk to hand out to a bunch of ravenous students who acted like they hadn't eaten in days. This included Fenn, who snatched his prize out of the air when it came flying his way—despite getting the wrong answer, since it was impossible for Ms. Galdamme to be only two years old. He tore open the wrapper, rudely tossed it to the floor, then shoved the whole thing in his mouth.

Chit-chit.

"Fenn, slow down," Miz told her friend as she watched him gobble up his treat. "You'll choke if you eat like that. Besides, you're being gross." She was about to remind him about the time last year when he'd choked on a bite of hot dog, and how his face had turned all sorts of funny colors, and how she'd smacked him on the back until a teacher rushed over to help. But when she looked down at the floor…

She froze.

A shiver went up her back when she noticed the small puddle of pee. Her best friend had a rather embarrassing problem under his desk, though he didn't seem to care.

"*Pssst.* Fenn!" Miz waved her hand down low, trying to avoid detention on her first day. She needed to get his attention before some of the other students found out. If Mike Tulette or one of his friends saw the mess, they'd bug him about it endlessly.

Miz snapped her fingers to get Fenn's attention. When that failed, she tried to whistle. But she was never any good at it. In a final effort to draw his gaze away from the teacher handing out treats for wrong answers, she stretched out her left leg and tapped her foot on the floor next to his desk.

Nobody seemed to pay any attention. The students only had eyes for the teacher, Ms. Galdamme.

Many students were bouncing in their seat like they had to go to the bathroom. Some of them *had*. Small puddles were under more desks than not, so it wasn't just her friend who'd had an accident.

And those *feet*.

Fenn's toes seemed extra long. A sharp nail attached to each chubby digit. Had his feet grown that much over the summer? When was the last time he cut his toenails?

"Good job, class! You might be the smartest students I've had in a long time," Ms. Galdamme was saying.

When the teacher returned to her desk to grab another handful of treats to hand out, Miz took the opportunity to reach across the aisle and flick her friend on the ear.

Fenn flinched in surprise. He rubbed his ear where he'd been hit, finally acknowledging her. But only so he could pass her a folded note.

Surprised, Miz quickly palmed the note before the teacher caught her being sneaky. Then she reached out her hand again for another note, and another. Two more in-class communications came from different sides. The last two notes were from Mike Tulette and Tracey Tispe, passed along by a few helpful students.

"Okay class, here's a tricky one," Ms. Galdamme said. "Which is smarter…rats or humans?"

"Rats!" cheered several students, who all received a prize, whether right or not.

As discreetly as she could, Miz unfolded all four notes and spread them out on her lap. It took far too much time to organize them, but when the words finally made sense, it was the same odd phrase from the filthy bathroom aboard the train.

WELCOME TO THE RAT RACE

The train, Miz thought, as if a fog had just lifted in her mind. *I need to get back to the train.*

It was already too late for that.

"A-*hem*."

A shadow fell over Miz, who simultaneously stiffened in her seat, drew a quick breath, and crunched up all the notes in her lap. She tried to hide them from the teacher, but had obviously been caught doing something she shouldn't have been doing in class.

"And you, my dear, must be Mizabella," said Ms. Galdamme, who had her glasses pulled down to the end of her nose so she could study her new pupil. The smile was still detectable, but it was more of a toothy grin that seemed to stretch unnaturally wide.

And those *eyes*.

Pretty by most standards, Ms. Galdamme also possessed the ability to use her unblinking stare to make the receiver feel intensely uncomfortable, or even threatened.

Miz felt a slight burn on her cheeks because the whole class was watching now. "No. I mean—yes." She forced herself to look the teacher directly in the eyes, despite the knowledge she was in trouble. "Actually, everyone just calls me Miz."

Ms. Galdamme tilted her head to one side, as if deciding what to do with the ill-behaved student.

Miz withdrew her gaze.

With surprising speed, the teacher suddenly seized her by the wrist, clamping down so hard that Miz could no longer conceal the secret in her hand, forced to allow her fingers to unfold and reveal the notes.

"Okay, *Miz*," said Ms. Galdamme, smiling wide enough to expose two short rows of unhealthy-looking teeth, stained brown and black. "I have a question for you. A nice, easy one." She swatted away the crumpled notes from her student's hand and let them drop to the floor. While thinking up a question, one long finger went *tap-tap-tap* on her chin.

No, not tapping. More like…scratching.

From her seat, Miz couldn't help but notice the large, cringe-worthy mole underneath the teacher's chin. Had it been there before? Or the patches of hair? What looked like a full chest of thick hair sprouted from under the collar of the teacher's STIGG MIDDLE SCHOOL t-shirt.

"Hmm, let's see…" Ms. Galdamme chattered her teeth together, grinding them. "Oh, I know! Miz, can you tell me how many victims perished during the Great Mortality between the years 1346 and 1353?"

Miz gave an embarrassed shrug. "Sorry. The…what? I don't think I know that one. What is it again?"

"The Black Plague, dear," said Ms. Galdamme, whose voice was soft and gentle as she tightened her grip on Miz's wrist, hard enough to make the student wince in pain. "You know, the Great Pestilence. All I'm asking is for you to tell me—and the whole class—how many people died during the world's worst pandemic."

Everyone was watching now. But not a single student—including her friends, Fenn and Reiny—seemed the least bit concerned that the teacher was being abusive to a student, grabbing her small wrist and squeezing it so tightly that it felt like the skin might peel away. Their large, round eyes—some black or brown, some bright pink—were focused on the small, shiny, silver package in the teacher's other hand.

"Um, ten thousand?" Miz guessed, then let out a sigh of relief when the teacher released the pressure on her wrist, but did not let go. Her heart was thumping so hard that she was sure the teacher could hear it.

"Good job, Miz! Good job." Ms. Galdamme dropped the prize into the student's hand, then finally let go.

"Thanks." Miz rubbed her sore wrist while the rest of the class looked on with a hungry look in their eyes, and fat, swollen tongues that dashed out, *thip-thip-thip*, then disappeared behind four sharp incisors.

Those *faces*.

The students were twitching in their seats, unable to sit still as they watched, curious and excited.

"Actually, Miz, the correct answer is somewhere between seventy-five and two hundred million," said Ms. Galdamme from the front of the classroom. "That's how many people perished during the Black Plague. And can you tell me the cause of it all?"

Though her mind was still foggy, Miz thought she may have heard somewhere that the cause of death of all those people was…

"Rats?"

Ms. Galdamme shook her head. "Although that is a common myth…that rats were the main carriers of *Yersinia pestis*, a deadly bacterium…it was actually humans who caused the disease to transfer so quickly. Not rats."

Miz choked out a weak response. "Oh. Sorry."

"Perhaps if you weren't so busy passing notes during class and distracting the other students, you wouldn't answer such simple questions with such stupid answers. Everyone else in class seems to know the right answers, except for *you*, Miz."

Miz felt the chill of a cold sweat on her arms and face. She had never been spoken to like this. Not by anybody, *ever.* And certainly not by a teacher. At a time like this, when she should stick up for herself, her mind had gone numb. Her legs felt weak. She felt hopeless at the hands of a cruel teacher who had seemed so nice a moment ago.

Ms. Galdamme spread out her arms, gesturing to all the other students in class. "Rats are our friends. *Your* friends, Miz. Take a look around and see all the friendly faces seated next to you. You have lots of friends here."

She was right.

Each student had changed—or was in the process of changing—into a nightmarish version of themselves. Not the kind of rodent you might see in the street, or scampering away under a bush, or diving into the sewer. These rats were the size of sixth-graders. Human faces, but with the features of a rat. Whiskers, twitchy nose, and a worm-like tail laying on the floor.

Chit-chit-chit!

Hands folded in her lap, squeezing them tightly to stop them from shaking, Miz was suddenly aware that she might end up with a puddle of pee under *her* desk if she didn't get away from here soon.

Fenn, Reiny, *everyone…*

Rats.

And the biggest, ugliest rat of them all was standing on

two legs up at the front of the classroom, ready to continue the lesson, as if everything was okay.

Worst of all, the school day had only just started.

CHAPTER 10

The day's lesson began with Ms. Galdamme explaining to her chattering students how, in her class, it would be impossible to fail. And how every answer would be awarded with a prize. Candy, extra free time, or something from the special prize drawer in her desk.

"There are no wrong answers," Ms. Galdamme said. "In this classroom, every answer is the right answer. You will all grow up to be selfish, lonely, empty individuals. So the best way to achieve that goal is with constant praise for a job poorly done."

Miz made a noise in the back of her throat. It wasn't directed at the teacher, but at her best friend, who was now also a rat. Fenn's eyes had turned big, round, and as black as the bottle of India ink on her art table back home.

"How about you, Miz?" Ms. Galdamme picked at her lips, where a row of pink bumps had appeared. "Do you understand?"

Miz choked out, "Yes, Ms. Galdamme."

"Class? How about the rest of you?"

Desks rattled on the floor.

Thump, thump, thump.

"Yes, Ms. Galdamme!" shouted the rest of the class, whose faces now hardly resembled her classmates.

Ms. Galdamme gave them a wide grin full of long, discolored teeth. "Good job, class! Good job." Her tail swept back and forth on the floor as she wrote PEMDAS on the board, about to launch into a math lesson.

Miz remembered that the funny acronym stood for: parentheses, exponents, multiplication, division, addition, subtraction. But wasn't there something else? Some forgotten detail? Her thoughts, foggy and unfocused since the moment she'd sat down, had completely wandered away from the fact that she needed to find a way out of this infested classroom. If she stayed much longer, she'd end up just like her rat friends.

"As you can see, class, inside the brackets is the equation seven times nine," said the creature that used to be Ms. Galdamme. "Can anyone tell me the correct answer? What is seven multiplied by nine?"

"Eleven!" hollered Tracey Tispe.

"Fifteen!" said Reiny.

"Blue!" shouted Fenn.

In this distorted classroom, all were correct.

"Good job, class! Good job." Ms. Galdamme had run out of mystery white Airheads candy, so she was now handing out full-sized boxes of SweeTARTS as a prize for each wrong answer. Most answers weren't even close, making less sense as the lesson progressed.

Miz sat obediently in her desk. Too scared to move, or even raise her hand to ask if she could use the bathroom, she was forced to listen as Ms. Galdamme continued to say many things.

Familiar things.

Concepts that Miz herself had dreamed up.

These were *her* ideas, being acted out in real life.

Miz would often sit in class and wish how no student would ever get the wrong answer. And how that would save them from any embarrassment. Or feeling bad about themselves. Or being subjected to verbal abuse from someone like Mike Tulette, who rarely had the right answer when called upon, but who loved to holler "Stooopid!" or some other clever comment whenever a student got the wrong answer.

What if all kids felt safe at school? What if teachers handed out treats for every answer? Even the wrong answer. Wouldn't that be great?

No, Miz thought. *It wasn't great.*

Because it wasn't real.

There *were* wrong answers in life.

The mind-fog had lifted enough that a plan was soon forming. Not a great plan, but it was all she had.

Miz quietly slid out of her desk.

This is where imaginations come to die.

Rattus' words echoed in her mind as she crawled on all-fours, down the aisle, carefully stepping over, around, and sometimes *through* the puddles of rat pee on the floor. The smell was the powerful, nose-curling scent of ammonia. Miz breathed as little as possible as she sneaked past all the desks, thankful she wore no shoes. They might squeak on the floor and draw unwanted attention.

"Good job, class! Good job."

More treats, more wrong answers.

When she'd safely reached the end of the aisle, Miz took a quick left and part bear crawled, part belly crawled along the back of the classroom.

The teacher, who no longer resembled the Ms. Galdamme that had first walked into the classroom, was too distracted by writing unintelligible scribbles on the whiteboard, or congratulating another student's bizarre answer and tossing them a prize for no reason.

"What is the most invasive species on the planet?"

"People!"

"What do they taste like?"

"Stink bugs!"

Tracey Tispe's thick tail shot out and smacked Miz in the stomach so hard that she hit the floor, gasping for air. Whether it was done intentionally or not, Miz couldn't tell. Clutching her midsection, she continued to inch her way toward the door, staying as low as possible to avoid being seen. She was certain the teacher would notice the empty desk, and quickly discover a student attempting to sneak away.

Somehow…she made it.

Rising up on two shaky legs that hardly felt like her own, much filthier (and smellier) than when she'd first entered the school, Miz felt a sudden burst of hope when she caught a glimpse of freedom just outside the open classroom door.

The exit down the hall.

All she had to do now was make it to the front door of the school and everything would be okay. She could escape this distorted version of the middle school and get back to the train. And to Rattus, who had hopefully figured out a way for her to get back home.

They can't hurt me, Miz thought. *They're just bits and pieces of my imagination.*

"Ms. Galdamme?"

The whole class turned around in their desks. Clicking

teeth, jaws grinding, and long tongues wagging side to side. Two dozen pairs of large, black, watery eyes void of any emotion stared at her like she was on the menu.

Chit-chit-chit-chit!

A distorted voice said, "Yeeeeeees?"

What Miz had conjured up in her mind to be the perfect sixth grade teacher had changed into something worse than any monster that Fenn—the *real* one, not the rat version—had ever come up with.

"I, uh…" Miz felt her stomach drop when the teacher turned to face her, with its cluster of eyes closed, using its horrific nose to sniff her out.

"Going somewhere, Miz?"

The pretty young teacher that used to be Ms. Galdamme now stood on two bony legs attached to a pair of wide feet, clawed and shaped like a shovel. Its pudgy body was covered in thick, matted fur, but still wearing the STIGG MIDDLE SCHOOL t-shirt. Her glasses had fallen off her misshapen face, at the end of which was a ring of pink tentacles, all wiggling and squirming and tasting the air to find its next meal. She was as ugly as the poster on the wall right next to her with the caption:

Meet the Star-nosed Canadian Mole!
The fastest eating mammal on Earth.

Miz had the strangest feeling that it was *her* imagination that made all this happen. Sitting in class, surrounded by students acting nice, being kind, and showing respect to one another for a change…her vivid imagination had somehow gotten away from her. Her thoughts had become polluted enough to turn all the students into rats, then change the perfect teacher into a monster. And now she couldn't change it back.

Sniff.

The creature that used to be Ms. Galdamme took a few shaky steps forward, sniffing the air, using its acute sense of smell to pinpoint the misbehaving student.

"Stay with us, Miz," said the teacher, whose garbled voice sounded like she was speaking through a mouth full of dirt. "Stay with your friends."

"Yeah, Miz. *Staaaaay.*"

"Don't go, Miz."

Reiny and Fenn begged her not to leave. Their voices were as unrecognizable as their faces. Soon all the rat students were pleading with her. Telling her not to go. Begging her to sit back down and join them. To win a prize for getting the wrong answer.

"Oh, Miz? Over here, sweetie!" Selected from her special prize drawer, the tentacled-faced teacher held up a selection of meats, unappetizing and covered in spots. Miz's stomach turned as her sixth grade teacher allowed the slimy, infectious meats to drip through her clawed fingers.

"Rotten fish? Putrid poultry? Moldy meat? See anything you like, dear? All my students see something *they* like."

Through its round mouth filled with at least forty jagged teeth, the horribly altered teacher sang a miserable song with no melody.

A class full of children
All bouncing in their seat
One jumped up and said,
'What's to eat?'

Following along in an eerie chorus, the entire class of rats sang their favorite part of the song, always reserved for the ones who'd mistakenly wandered into their midst.

Is it a child? Is it a pest?
Can it run faster than the rest?
Nibble on his feet
Nibble on her face
Soon we'll know just how it
Tastes!

"Well, class? What do you say we all take a short break from lessons and have a quick bite to eat?" said the creature that was once Ms. Galdamme.

The rat that used to be her best friend Reiny was the first to rise from her desk. Fenn, Mike Tulette, Tracey Tispe, and the rest of them stood up too. All were a bit shaky on their feet, as if still getting used to their new rodent bodies.

Turning to face the escaping student, the teacher's mouth opened extra wide and said in a wretched voice, "What do you taste like, *Miiiiiz*?"

Chit-chit-chit went those awful teeth.

The last thing she heard before rushing from the classroom was the sound of desks scraping on the floor. Then a flurry of padded feet scurrying as the excitable rats chased down the tasty young student that had just raced from the room.

"Come back!" the rats cried.

"Stay here, Miz!"

Miz bolted down the hallway. She passed the football trophies, then burst through the big double door and raced outside.

Thump.

Two dozen large rats collided with the heavy door.

As Miz stumbled backwards, thankful to be outside but still unable to take her eyes off the bouncing, biting, scratching, clawing rat students who climbed all over each other, she heard a soft *click* as the door opened.

The race was on.

Miz hurried down the steps, then along the slanted

concrete pathway. The only thing that prevented her from being overtaken by a pack of sixth grade rodents was the small distraction she'd left behind, where the concrete ended and the field of mud began.

Her shoes.

With no idea which way was the right direction, Miz picked one and ran. She was nowhere near fast enough to outrun a pack of sugared up rats who had already ripped apart her shoes, eaten them, and were still hungry for more.

Ooooooo.

Somewhere out in the heavy fog came the sound of the train's horn. The low moan carried across the muddy landscape.

Miz could hear the high-pitched hiss of steam, followed by the *whump-whump-whump* as the train engine rumbled to life. Her ride was about to leave without her.

"Rattus!" Miz yelled. "Wait for me!"

When she broke through the trees and saw the vague outline of the train, she sprinted with every ounce of energy she had left. Her lungs burned and her throat felt like a sandbox. But the fear of what would happen when the rats caught up to her was more than enough to keep her charging ahead, while the mud and filth kicked up from her pumping legs continued to splatter into her face, eyes, and everywhere else.

Ignoring the foul taste in her mouth, Miz darted toward the open platform door.

The rats were gaining.

Over the sound of her own feet squelching in the mud, Miz heard the *splat-splat-splat* of two dozen rat-faced sixth graders closing in on her. Every one of them was eager to feed.

"Rattus! HELP!" Miz screamed, but there was no sign of her rodent friend. Not that he would be much help, since the rats chasing her were much bigger than the average sewer dweller.

Splat.

Miz tripped and fell over, sinking elbow deep into the sea of filth. She pulled herself out and kept running. With only a short distance left to reach the train, the rats would overwhelm her long before she made it to the open door.

Just ten yards from the train, she made a foolish decision to test out an equally foolish plan.

Miz stopped running.

The rats stopped too. Clever as well as hungry, they quickly formed a semi-circle around the flighty meal.

Clenched tightly in her muddy fist was the prize she'd won earlier, when Ms. Galdamme awarded her for answering incorrectly about the Black Death.

Rats crave sugar as much as anyone.

"Here!" Miz held the small silver package high in the

air. "You want it?" She waved it slowly back and forth until she had the attention of every chittering, chattering, squealing rat.

Chit-chit-chit-chit!

Twenty-four sets of teeth clicked, while twenty-four sets of black, hungry eyes tracked the movement of the sugary prize.

"Then go get it!" Miz launched the candy as far as she could. Not very far, but enough to give her a chance to get to the train while the pack of sixth grade rats raced through the mud, clawing, biting, and fighting each other to be the first to find it.

Slam!

Miz closed the train door, but the broken latch dangled uselessly to the side, forcing her to hold the door shut. Through the small round window in the door, she could see all the rats fighting over the treat. Only one or two got to enjoy a bite. Realizing they'd been tricked, the rats raced toward the train car.

Ooooooo.

The train lurched forward. Miz climbed up the four steps and into the passenger car, where she found a small, confused sewer rat staring back at her.

"Where have you been?" Rattus was up on the table, busy munching on what looked like the skeletal remains of a rotted fish. "Off having an adventure without me, eh?

Oh well." He sniffed. "Look what I found?" He proudly held up the dead fish. "The train doesn't have a dining car, but I discovered this little beauty hiding in an overturned bucket a few cars down. Care to join me?"

Miz dropped heavily into the booth, slid across the seat toward the cracked, dirty window, and carefully pressed her nose up to the glass and looked down.

Twenty-four rat faces peered up.

"What's wrong?" Rattus stopped eating and stuck his small, furry face up to the window next to her.

Chit-chit-chit.

"Ah, I see," Rattus said, equally fascinated by all the hungry faces staring up at them, scratching at the metal as they attempted to climb aboard. "Ugly, aren't they? Some of them might be big enough to give the Grundt a bit of trouble—perhaps."

"Come on, come on..." Miz pounded a fist on the table, willing the train to move faster. Their only escape was moving dreadfully slow, chugging and puffing and spewing black smoke into the air—a signal that this might be its final ride down the tracks.

"Can't this train move any faster?" Miz was worried the clever rats would figure out how to open the passenger door, get inside, then proceed to...feast.

Whump, whump, whump.

"Yes!" Miz cheered quietly.

Through the dirty window, Miz watched as her old classmates—or *rat-mates*—soon gave up on the train, then raced each other back to the middle school, where a teacher with tentacles growing out of her face would hand out treats for a job poorly done.

Miz lay her head on the dusty table and took a minute to catch her breath. Reluctantly, she stood up, wincing at the pain in her abdomen.

"Now where are you going?" Rattus asked with a bit of fish bone jutting out from the side of his mouth.

Now that the rats were safely behind them, Miz's body had a chance to recover. The pressure on her bladder made it feel like she'd swallowed a five-pound hairball.

Over her shoulder, Miz said, "I'll be back in a minute." She shivered at the thought of where she was headed, then said, "I guess I don't have a choice but to use that nasty bathroom in the next train car."

Rattus went too, right where he was.

CHAPTER 11

Sitting in a dirty train booth and retelling the story of her miserable first day of middle school made the tiny hairs on her arms stand up. Images of giant rat kids chasing after her and a teacher with pink tentacles growing out of her face brought an instant queasy feeling to her stomach (and dread at the thought of having to use the train bathroom again). Those faces would haunt her dreams.

"It was like being stuck inside a movie," Miz explained. "Except most of the time I was too scared to move, or talk, or do anything—except run away. I probably could've stood up to them, but I just—" She hung her head. "It all happened so fast."

"Mm," said Rattus, which could have been a reply or a

satisfied grunt after enjoying a bite of his tasty rotted fish.

Miz was glad the nightmare classroom visit was over, but also disheartened to be back inside a broken-down passenger train. She was also grateful to her only friend in this place for lending an ear, even if they were the tiny shriveled ears of a sewer rat. Still, the awful stench of his lunch could not be ignored any longer.

"Can you get rid of that, please?" Miz pointed to the fish remains that had her plugging her nose.

"Oh, fine. Be that way," Rattus said grudgingly, but still obliged. Without much left to enjoy anyway, he used his forepaws to push the unfinished meal to the edge of the table, nibbling the last little bits as he went, then dropped the rotten mess to the floor. It didn't help much with the foul odor, but at least the dead fish was out of sight.

"Thanks." Miz scratched her rat friend behind his ears. He seemed to like it, so she kept doing it until she felt more like herself again—still lost, but not sinking into an emotional pit, feeling hopeless. Like she *belonged* here.

"Maybe having a big imagination isn't such a good thing after all," she told the rat. "Maybe I should just grow up and act like everybody else. My brother isn't creative anymore, but he's going off to college to get a business degree. My parents aren't creative at all, and they've both got pretty good jobs. What if being creative and loving art as much as I do is a big waste of time? Maybe I should take up a different hobby, like sending emails or staring at home decor websites."

Rattus dropped onto his furry backside to stare out the train window alongside his grumpy traveling companion.

"Hey, cheer up," Rattus said. "Even sewer dwellers like me can sometimes see the light at the end of the drainage pipe of life." He'd never come up with anything this profound before, so was rather proud of himself.

Miz groaned. "Not helpful."

Rattus tried again. "Okay, look—this is where unused imaginations come to dwell once they are discarded," he reminded her. "The place where imaginations come to die."

"I know," Miz said. "You already told me that."

"Yes, but don't forget that *your* imagination is still active," Rattus reminded her. "That's because you use it every day, so it still belongs to you. And yet, somehow…"

"What?" Miz asked.

"Things here can become a little distorted," Rattus said as he cleaned his whiskers. "I suppose this place is a bit like a clear blue lake that has become polluted over time. What may have started out as a perfect picture in your mind—such as your first day of middle school—may not end well in the dwelling place of lost imaginations."

"Yeah, I'll say." Miz shook her head to clear it of the awful images replaying in her mind. "That was the worst school day ever."

"Ah, but remember…" Rattus held up one forepaw like he was about to say something important, then sunk his teeth into his underarm to stop the incessant itching. Finally, he raised his paw again to speak, the itch satisfied.

"Even a polluted lake can be cleaned up. Returned, if you like, to its natural state. Rescued, I suppose."

"Yeah, maybe." Miz lay her head down on her arms and stared out the one clean spot on the window as the train rumbled down the tracks. "But how do you rescue somebody's imagination?"

Rattus didn't know either.

Outside the train window, the fog had lifted—if only a little. The steady line of treetops were black and symmetrical, as if the same pattern repeated itself, mile after mile. What could be hills, or even mountains, appeared way off in the distance. That was about as much as Miz could make out in this vacant land.

Dozens of wrought-steel wheels continued to grind along the tracks, shaking and rattling and making for a very bumpy ride. The steady noise and movement had caused the smaller of the two passengers to doze off.

Rattus had fallen asleep on the table, curled up into a

furry ball. His tiny legs kicked out every once in a while, possibly running away from something frightful in his dreams. Or perhaps he was reliving the nightmare when his girlfriend nibbled on—nibbled *off*—his poor toes.

About to doze off herself, Miz knew she should be busy dreaming up a way out of this place. But all she could do was sit and think about losing a friend—a best friend, Reiny. They'd done everything together, since childhood. Then *poof*, it was gone. Their longtime friendship was over.

Her thoughts also drifted to her brother, and how he used to be so creative, sitting and drawing with her for hours on rainy days. She felt that it was a terrible tragedy how people so often, all of sudden, one day…change.

Another huge worry was middle school. Would the teachers be patient and understanding? Or would they be cruel and demanding? Maybe they'd push their students too hard, handing out test, after test, after test. Will there be so much homework that it would drain all her free time? Would she be forced to crunch math numbers and read boring text books instead of making art up in her room?

It made her stomach cramp up to think that Fenn, her only artistic friend left, may drift away too.

Did attending middle school mean she would have to start all over and find new friends? Would any of them be creative? Or would they all be into things like clothes and makeup, just so boys would talk to them?

Miz could feel herself sinking. If she sunk much further, the cushion spring digging into her backside would break the skin, and possibly cause an infection.

Ooooooo.

The train's sad whistle blew again. This time it was loud enough to wake up the snoozing rat.

"So?" Rattus sat up after a nice yawn and a stretch, then crawled over to sit next to his travel mate. He curled up right next to her folded arms to give the appearance of being friendly. Really, he was just trying to steal some of her body heat.

"So what?" Miz said in a snarky voice that didn't sound much like her at all. Stuck in such a dismal place with no idea how to get back, she felt so low that she didn't want to do anything but keep riding the train to nowhere.

"Where would you like to try next?" Rattus asked, trying to sound uplifting for both their sakes. "Exploring the middle school was obviously a bad choice, but you never know—the next stop could be your ticket home!"

Miz pulled herself up off the table. Just enough to rest her head in her hands. "Forget it. I just had the worst experience of my life," she said, unable to shake the visions of hungry rats closing in on her. Jaws clicking. Those horrible, high-pitched squeaks ringing in her ears. Sights and sounds she may never forget. "I don't think I want to stop anywhere else."

Rattus slumped onto his furry backside, then scratched himself. "Well, we can't just keep riding this lonely train forever. You'll have to eat at some point, won't you? And that tiny bit of delicious rotten fish was all I could find on the whole train." As if having his point inadvertently proven, he heard the girl's stomach growl.

Miz *was* hungry. Starving, actually. Walking through a muddy field one way, then being chased the other way had taken its toll—mentally and physically. The stomach pangs grew worse as the train rumbled on.

"What's the point?" Miz said. "This place is polluted, right? A distorted version of my own imagination. So even if I imagine some new place…a *good* place…it'll just turn out bad." She sighed. "Just like that classroom full of disgusting rats."

Rattus stopped biting his itchy skin.

"Sorry," Miz said with an embarrassed shrug. "I didn't mean it like that."

"Not to worry," Rattus said, unhurt. Thoughtfully, he asked, "Where would you normally go after a bad day at school? There must be some place safe." He let out a chirpy squeak. "Some of those afterschool recreation buildings, the YMCA and such, oftentimes have the most delightful dumpsters to dig through." His black eyes seemed to glaze over. "All those lovely blue bins loaded with half-eaten lunches, bread crusts, yogurt containers…"

Miz knew the answer right away.

Just a short walk from her old school was a safe place. The best place in the world, where she and her friends used to go after school at least twice (sometimes three or four times) a week. And always on Fridays. A place that smelled of lemon-scented Pine-Sol, mothballs, and Clorox, but always had the best fresh baked goodies imaginable.

"Grammy's house."

Rattus' ears pricked up. "Ooh, a grammy?" His small, worm-like tongue flitted out the sides of his mouth. "Is that anything like those delicious graham wafers I sometimes find in neighborhood trash bins?"

Miz gave a small laugh. "My grandma's house," she explained. "Me, Fenn, and Reiny used to walk to Grammy's house all the time after school, so we could stuff ourselves on snacks and pop. On Fridays, Grammy always had fresh baked cookies, or cake, or some new recipe she'd pick out from one of her ten thousand cookbooks."

Rattus' greedy eyes sparkled. Then he nearly fell off the table when the train gave a vicious jolt.

Chuff-chuff-chuff.

"Oof!" Miz took the full brunt of the heavy table when the last bolt holding it to the floor came loose. Surprised by the weight of the faux marble table, it took her three tries to push it the opposite way. When she finally managed to get it shoved off her chest, allowing her to take a full breath, she accidentally shoved too hard the other way. The whole thing teetered on its edge, then began to topple over into the aisle.

Squeak!

Rattus' claws dug uselessly into the cracked marble tabletop as he skidded backwards, squeaking for help as he slid toward the edge. The heavy tabletop broke free of its metal post, then crashed to the floor with a thud. The cloud of dust made Miz cough, but also distracted her enough to forget what she was holding in her hand.

"Thanks," Rattus said, hanging upside-down.

Miz had never held a rat by its tail. But since it was the only thing within reach as her small friend slid off the table, she'd grabbed onto his dry, lumpy tail.

"You're welcome," she said, then gently (but quickly) placed the rat back on the floor, doing so while ignoring the cringy feeling in her stomach and the goosebumps going clear up her arms from holding a sewer dweller. "I didn't want you to get squished under the table."

Rattus used his strong hind legs to jump up on the seat opposite of Miz, where he immediately stuck his nose in between the seat cushions in search of any stale crumbs or bits of food left behind. Finding none, he slumped down on the seat like a weary traveler who'd just had his hopes trampled on.

"At least now we have more room to sit and talk, right?"

Rattus clicked his teeth. "But without a table between us, I'm afraid we won't be able to play cards."

Miz gave him a look. "That was a joke, right?"

Rattus scratched himself as he stared lazily at the girl across the booth. "That," he declared, "was a joke."

The train car rattled and the brakes squealed horribly loud, but the rundown locomotive was slowing down.

"Rattus, look!" Miz shoved her face up to the window so fast that her nose bounced painfully off the glass. Rubbing her nose, she gazed out the window, eyes wide as they took in all the wonderful sights that seemed like a distant dream. The world outside had cleared up.

Intensely blue sky.

Urban forest.

Houses, cars, and people.

Couples were out for a stroll, or walking their dogs, while grumpy old men mowed their lawn and mumble-cursed at all the kids out playing and having fun in the sun.

"Wait a second. I know this street," Miz said. "This *can't* be right. Can it? We're at my—" Her heart lifted as she soaked up the sight of a welcoming, safe place.

"Let me guess," Rattus said, rubbing his greedy forepaws together. "This is your grandmother's street, correct? And I'm assuming that mid-century home with the beige trim and carefully tended shrubs and flowers over there is your beloved Grammy's house?"

Miz nodded, unable to believe her luck. This stop wasn't anything like the foggy, muddy, miserable scene outside the middle school. This was a gorgeous summer day! White clouds danced across the blue sky. Happy families were outside enjoying the sunshine. And lots of kids—some she even recognized—were riding bikes and scooters and electric cars.

Thunk.

The train rolled to a stop. When the engine shut off, making all sorts of strange noises, the whole train shuddered like it was giving its dying breath, then went silent.

Same as before, the rusty door creaked open, as if the train was kicking her off again.

"Shall I go with you?" Rattus asked. "I may be small, but I can be quite brave." He paused, then looked down at his missing toes. "Well…sometimes."

Miz hadn't thought about it, but quickly agreed. In this place, she would definitely appreciate the company.

"Are you sure you want to come with me?" she asked the rat. "It might not be safe out there. What if it's the middle school all over again?"

Rattus let out a chirpy squeak and scratched his paws in the air, begging to be lifted up and carried.

Miz picked up the rat. When her furry friend wiggled aggressively in her hands, she steeled herself as he climbed up the length of her arm, right up to her shoulder. She could feel tiny claws digging into her bare skin, but not enough to cause any damage.

"There were go," Rattus said, now perched up high like a king rat. "A much better view from up here. Onwards! Lead the way. To Grammy's house we must go!"

Down the steps, about to exit through the passenger door with the little round window, Miz was having second thoughts about getting off the train, while her rat friend pestered her about what kinds of food he might soon be tempted with at Grammy's house.

"What are you waiting for?" Rattus was ready to stuff himself with so many goodies that he would have to be carried around.

"I—I don't know." Miz hesitated on the bottom step. She shouldn't have gotten off the train the last time, to traipse across a field of mud, only to end up in a classroom full of rats, led by a horrific teacher with a tentacle mouth. That time, she'd been so eager to get somewhere else that she was willing to take the risk.

Rattus sniffed the air, able to use his powerful olfactory to pick up the delectable scent of baking.

"Ahh," he said. "Smells like…cookies."

Miz was just shy of talking herself out of what could be another nightmare in disguise. An imagination trap.

Just then, the front door of the house across the street

opened. An elderly woman wearing an oversized, faded green sweater and loose-fitting white pants stepped out onto the front porch.

"Hi-ya, sweetie!" a familiar voice called. "How was school today? Did you learn anything good?"

Less than fifty steps from the train, up the driveway and past the flower garden, a white-haired lady waved with one hand, while the other held a baking sheet full of goodies pulled fresh from the oven.

"Grammy!" Miz gave an excited wave in return. Her mud-caked, shoeless feet were down the steps, off the train, and rushing up the driveway for a quick visit.

CHAPTER 12

Aside from the broken-down locomotive taking up most of Skummelt Avenue, everything looked exactly like the last time she'd visited. Houses with hardly any variety of color stretched up and down the block. Shiny cars and SUVs sat parked in driveways or out on the road, where most windshields were littered with fallen leaves, twigs, and plenty of bird droppings from all the chubby robins that lived in the high branches.

The tall trees provided plenty of shade for the kids who were always out playing, screaming obnoxiously loud, and causing mischief.

"We'll have to watch out for her," Miz said as she pointed out the young girl who lived a few houses down. "That's Avery, the neighborhood terror."

Sitting in the driver's seat of a hot pink Land Rover, a motorized car that could be used as a weapon, was a three-year-old girl wearing a fancy dress and a plastic tiara that sat crooked atop her long blonde hair. She always had the wickedest grin on her round face, especially whenever unsuspecting older kids came walking down the sidewalk, on their way home from school.

"If you're not careful, she'll sneak up behind you and bash her toy car into the back of your legs," Miz explained. She hoped to go unnoticed as she exited the train and headed toward Grammy's house.

"Hopefully *your* legs," said Rattus. "Not mine."

"I've been hit by her a few times." Miz laughed to herself while thinking back to just a few short months ago, when Miss Avery had snuck up on Fenn (while she and Reiny had kept quiet, of course, knowing what was about to happen) and bashed her faux yuppy vehicle into the back of his legs. Fenn screamed in the upper tenor range as he was chased down the sidewalk by a giggling toddler driving a toy car at a blazing 5 MPH.

"Where'd she go?" Miz asked.

"Who? The bad driver in the pink car?" Rattus flicked a paw down the sidewalk. "She's hiding behind that tree. And, I might add, she is looking this way."

"No, Grammy." While attempting to sneak across the road and up the driveway without being struck from behind, her grandma had gone back inside the house. Usually she would wait on the porch, ready to give her only granddaughter one of her bone-squishing hugs before inviting them into the house.

Miz shrugged it off. "The oven timer must've beeped," she said to the rat carefully balanced on her shoulder. "Grammy's always in the kitchen. Half the time she makes so much food that she ends up giving it to the neighbors. Everyone on this whole block gets to enjoy her cooking."

Rattus' entire body trembled with excitement at the mention of food. His greedy black eyes reflected the sunrays peeking through the trees. "Ah, now *those* are the types of houses that we rats love to visit late at night," he said wistfully. "Hiding between the walls, waiting for the indwellers to go to sleep." He'd spent many hours inside suburban homes, hiding in the shadows, waiting patiently until he could sneak into the cupboards after the house had gone quiet.

Miz cringed at the thought of rats in the walls. Did that include bedroom walls too? Bathroom walls?

"Takeout food is also good," Rattus went on. "Old pizza boxes with a bit of moldy cheese…buckets of greasy fried chicken with leftover bits of crunchy skin…or those little Chinese food containers with a few slimy noodles still at the bottom of the box. But nothing tastes better than home cooking."

Miz agreed. "You'll love Grammy's house."

Under the careful watch of the young princess girl who was peeking out from behind a tree, waiting for the perfect opportunity to strike, Miz hurried up the front porch steps, where she noticed something missing.

Her grandmother wasn't especially good at walking up steps anymore, so her dad had installed a ramp. An in-depth home project that involved him laying down a plank of wood across the steps to make it easier for her. It wasn't especially odd that the wooden board had been removed—perhaps by a friendly neighbor? Miz did recall seeing one of those easy-step canes in the hallway a few months ago, so thought nothing of it as she climbed the steps and stood politely at the front door.

Sniff.

"I detect the scent of vanilla," said Rattus as his nose twitched. "And marshmallows! And peanut butter, one of my favorites!"

"That's probably homemade fudge you smell," Miz told him as she wiped her muddy socks on the welcome mat. "Grammy makes the most amazing peanut butter fudge." She could feel the rat on her shoulder trembling with excitement. "Best in the world."

The door buzzer didn't seem to work, so Miz knocked on the open door.

"Grammy, it's us!" Miz hollered into the house.

"Door's open!" Grammy hollered back. "I'm in the kitchen, sweetie. Be right out with some goodies! I've tried a new recipe, so I hope you and your little friend brought your appetites!"

Down the hallway, turn left, then straight into the familiar living room. Miz plunked right down on Grammy's comfortable but excruciatingly ugly couch. Green and yellow plaid, complete with hand-stitched doilies and a plastic sheet in case of spills.

Miz felt safe here. Protected. And also hungry enough to eat anything put in front of her. Her poor stomach growled loudly enough to make her rat friend flinch.

"Sounds like you're as famished as me!" Rattus said. With a tremendous leap, he jumped clear off her shoulder. Skinny arms and thick legs (with toes nibbled off) spread wide, he landed with a soft *plop*, right on top of Grammy's polished glass coffee table.

Ding!

The kitchen timer buzzed, followed by the familiar shuffling, scuffling sounds of a master baker busy at work.

"I hope you're hungry!" Grammy called to them.

"Starving," Miz replied. "I've been having the weirdest morning, Grammy. This snobby girl I sort of know threw one of Fenn's best drawings into the sewer, so I went down to get it. Then I met this huge rat, and I—" She stopped, suddenly aware that she was probably saying too much.

Grammy didn't want to hear about disgusting sewers and a rat the size of a grown man. She was about to change the subject by asking where all the pictures and decorations had gone—all noticeably missing from the walls, end tables, and the mantel. But the smell of something wonderful suddenly filled the living room.

"Soda bread, anyone?" Grammy appeared in the doorway, holding a plate of dessert bread. Dressed in one of her usual oversized sweaters (the dark green one today), comfy white pants, and her light brown orthopedic shoes, she beamed at her only granddaughter.

"Yes, please." Miz rubbed her hands together, ready to try the new recipe. She'd never tried soda bread, but enjoyed the wonderful smell of food as Grammy placed the white frosting covered bread onto the coffee table, along with some drinks for her guests.

Rattus squeaked with delight. Without asking for permission, he scurried across the glass tabletop and attacked the round loaf of sweet bread.

Miz pointed to the rat on the table, who was gobbling up small pieces of bread as fast as his strong jaws and tough molars could grind it up.

"Don't worry, Grammy," she said. "He's with me. That's Rattus, my new friend. All he ever thinks about is food."

Grammy didn't seem to mind that a sewer rat had also

stopped by for a visit. "Well, I'm glad I baked enough for both of you!" She reached down to gently scratch her rat visitor behind the ears. "Oh my, aren't you a hungry little thing."

Rattus stopped stuffing his mouth long enough to give the woman's hand a quick sniff—a scent he recognized as well as his own skin. Satisfied, he went back to eating.

Grammy sat in her electric recliner without bothering to use the remote. Since her back always ached, the seat assist mechanism helped her sit down much easier. But today she didn't seem to need any help.

"Go on, Miz dear. Dig in!" Grammy said as she rocked slowly back and forth. "Have something to eat first, and then you can tell me all about your day."

Unable to resist any longer, Miz's empty stomach had her reaching for the plate of soda bread. After tearing off a fist-sized section of bread (from one of the few sections that Rattus had *not* touched with his dirty claws or licked with his wormy tongue), she began to nonchalantly pick off all the raisins and blackcurrants. She couldn't stand either one, but was too polite to say it.

Rattus had already done the same thing. "Don't eat those." He pointed a claw to his own small pile of raisins, or currant berries, or whatever they were. "Just eat the bread part."

Miz wished that she'd at least washed her hands, but

was too hungry to care. After she'd practically inhaled her food, she poured herself a glass of water from the pitcher on the table, then cringed as the odd-tasting water went down her throat. Tap water always tasted a bit off at Grammy's house, so today must be a *really* off-day. She poured herself a glass of lemonade instead.

"I apologize that I don't have any utensils for you to use, sweetie," Grammy said, then scratched at the side of her mouth, where a little red bump was visible on her cheek. "Everything's in the washing machine. You'll just have to use your hands, dear."

"That's okay, Grammy." Miz tore off another small section of bread. As hungry as she was, she didn't want to stuff herself too quickly and end up feeling sick. The first piece was already like a rock inside her stomach, so she ate the second piece much slower, grimacing when she accidentally bit down on one of the hard, crunchy berries she'd missed.

Rattus seemed to be laughing at her. He was too busy stuffing his face to say anything to warn her.

"How is it, hon?" Grammy asked.

"It's really good," Miz told her, though felt somewhat guilty for not being completely truthful. The berries left a horribly bitter aftertaste in her mouth. "You can definitely mark this page in your cookbook." To be polite, she picked out another small piece of soda bread, held it in her hand,

and pretended to nibble on it.

While Rattus continued to stuff himself, Miz sank comfortably into the couch. The living room was quiet. Quiet, cozy, and safe.

The gas fireplace was blazing away even though it was summertime. Beads of sweat formed on her forehead and under her arms. Miz considered asking if they could switch off the faux fire, or maybe turn down the thermostat. In the end, she decided against it, since most grandparents' houses she'd been in (Reiny's and Fenn's grandparents) were usually a bit stuffy. Seniors were always so cold, but always such good company.

Grammy rocked gently in her recliner. Her white hair looked especially thin today, and her eyes seemed a bit watery too. Probably just from being overjoyed whenever her only granddaughter (and friends) stopped by for a visit.

"So? How was your first day of middle school?" Grammy asked. "Did you like it? Were the teachers nice?"

Miz opened her mouth to answer, but couldn't think of a decent way to put it. A tentacle-mouthed teacher? Rat students? A whole class of rat kids chasing her down, clicking their teeth at her heels, ready to enjoy some *almuerzo de Miz*. How could she possibly explain all that?

Ding!

The oven timer went off again.

"That's for me!" Grammy sprang up out of the

recliner, much more spry than usual, and hurried into the kitchen, where she pulled another batch of fresh baked goodies from the oven. This time she came back to the living room carrying a sheet of oatmeal cookies with very large chocolate chips as big as Hershey's kisses.

Rattus' greedy black eyes noticed the plate of cookies hiding behind the loaf of bread. He'd basically eaten a tunnel through the soda bread, so he had to wriggle his body back out when he detected the scent of more delectable treats on the table.

"Hungry little fellow, isn't he?" Grammy said, rocking away in her recliner. Her frail hands (shaking worse than usual today) were folded neatly in her lap. She always looked so happy when her guests were enjoying the food she'd prepared.

"Yeah, part rat," Miz said, "and part pig. I've never seen something so little eat so much."

Rattus stopped eating long enough to glare at the girl, just for a second, then went back to stuffing himself with cookies. He especially enjoyed the large chocolate chips, cut into funny-shaped pieces.

Miz politely grabbed a cookie.

Ding!

"Off again!" Grammy hopped up from the chair and dashed off to the kitchen.

"Grammy, how much food are you making?" Miz said

with a laugh. "There are only two of us here today. But I guess Rattus counts as at least two by himself."

Rattus ignored her as he bit into a large, crunchy chocolate chip, gobbling it up in seconds.

When Miz finally realized what was missing from the living room—something that had been bugging her since she first sat down, but couldn't quite place it—she hollered into the kitchen, where the sounds of a mixer, clanging bowls, and the familiar *squeak* of the oven door opening and shutting filtered out.

"Grammy?"

"Yes, sweetie?"

"Where are all the pictures of Grandpa? And us?" Miz had her own special place atop the mantel, where a large framed photo of her was proudly displayed at all times, and updated with each new school picture. The family picture was missing too, taken when they all went camping— Mom, Dad, her brother, and Grammy too, back when she could move around a lot better. Miz was only a toddler at the time, too young to remember anything about the trip. And several old photographs of Grandpa, including the one of them outside the church where they were married, the one from his military service, and one from a fishing trip with just the two of them. All had been removed or packed away.

"Did you hire someone?" Miz asked. "Are they

painting the inside walls?" Her last living grandparent kept her home very tidy, and always had workers coming in and out, fixing things, installing some new light fixture, spraying for bugs, or doing yard work she could no longer do.

"Painting, dear?" Grammy looked confused when she came back into the living room carrying yet another dish. She looked to where her granddaughter was pointing, then shrugged. "Ah, I see what you mean."

"Redecorating, maybe?" Miz suggested.

"Yes, redecorating," Grammy said vacantly as she placed another large plate on the coffee table. She made sure not to drop it on the tail of the sewer rat, who seemed to love her food more than life itself. This time it was a three-layer dessert big enough to feed at least ten people.

A lopsided cake, dark brown.

Ding!

Grammy squealed excitedly and darted back into the kitchen.

Miz went to take a bite of her cookie, then made a face. Pulling on the thin black hair that was sticking out, she quickly realized it wasn't a hair after all.

It was an antenna.

"*Ugh*, sick!" Miz dropped the cookie on the floor. Not wanting to touch it again, but also not wanting to make a mess at her Grammy's house, she quickly picked it up and tossed it onto the table.

"No, thanks." Rattus held up what was left of his cookie. "I've got my own! See?"

Miz wiped her forehead with one of Grammy's hand-stitched doilies because (for once) there were no napkins, or even a box of tissues around. The steadily rising heat was becoming unbearable. Or was it something else? Something besides the hot house? And the odd-tasting food? And the missing pictures? And Grammy's vacant stare?

Miz gripped the edge of the sofa when it finally occurred to her that this may not be…accurate. The mind-fog had, once again, clouded her judgment. This might be a distorted version of Grammy's house. And if that was true, then she wondered who—or *what*—was in the kitchen making all the food.

"Pssst!" Miz hissed at her rat friend. He didn't seem worried at all that they might be in the middle of a dangerous trap—a rat's nest.

"Rattus," Miz whispered louder. "Rattus!" She didn't want to draw any unwanted attention, so after being ignored a third time, she picked him up by the tail.

"What's wrong?" Rattus asked, upside-down.

"We need to go," Miz said as she placed the rat back up on her shoulder. "Now," she told him, then stood up to leave.

"What—? Now? Why?" Rattus acted like he was being ripped away from a rat's dream come true. Half a cookie was clutched in his forepaws. He had crumbs on his face, stuck in his whiskers, and all over his furry body. "Who would ever want to leave such a place?"

"I'll tell you outside," Miz told him as she crept out of the living room and down the hall, tiptoeing on the carpet in her muddy socks.

"Aren't these cookies simply delicious?" Rattus took another scrumptious bite. "Beetles, a pinch of moth, a bit of centipede...yum!"

Miz put a hand to her mouth. *Bug cookies*, she thought. *That's what I've been eating.*

Stealthily creeping down the hallway, trying to make the least amount of noise possible, Miz held on to the rat who was greedily munching on the last bit of his cookie with the "special ingredients" inside.

Miz paused at the closet door by the foyer.

Since her imagination had conjured up most parts of the house correctly, pulled from her subconscious before being distorted and polluted, she recalled how her beloved Grammy let her only granddaughter keep an extra sweater, rain jacket, and a pair of mud boots at the house, just in case.

Miz scooped up the boots, then gasped.

A high-pitched scream came from the kitchen. The noise echoed through the whole house. There'd been some kind of accident.

"Oh!" Grammy cried.

Crash.

Miz's heart was thumping hard in her chest when she called out, "Grammy? Are you okay?" She had to fight the urge to rush into the kitchen to check on her frail grandmother, to see if she was all right.

"I'm fine, sweetie," Grammy said, suddenly appearing in the doorway. She was carrying another plate full of treats. "Everything is just fine, dear. Sit back down. Stay awhile. Stay with *meeeeee.*"

Miz gave a horrified scream.

The thing pretending to be her Grammy came stumbling down the hallway, walking on legs that seemed to bend in the wrong direction. One clawed hand reached up to stroke its long whiskers. Three on each side, jutting out of the big red bumps on her cheeks. Whiskers as thick as her finger, and at least two feet long.

"Peanut butter fudge, dear?" said Grammy-rat with a sinister look in her cold, black eyes.

Miz yelped when Rattus' sharp claws dug into her shoulder as she stumbled down the hall, inching her way toward the front door. His long tail kept smacking against her cheek while he hissed in her ear, urging her to move faster.

"Go on, sweetie," said Grammy-rat. "I know these are your favorite afterschool snack, *Miiiiz.*"

CHAPTER 13

Art had always been Miz's favorite subject in the world, but reading fantasy novels came in a close second. Many times while reading (or re-reading) one of her favorite books, she'd come across the phrase "knees knocking together" or something similar, and thought how funny it sounded. How nobody could ever be *that* scared.

"*Miiiiz*, honey? Come closer, dear…"

But seeing what just walked into the living room carrying a plate of "treats" had turned her blood icy cold. Her legs shook so badly that the insides of her knees smacked together like in all those stories.

"Sorry, Grammy, but I…" Miz took a few backward steps down the hallway, unable to pull her eyes away from the creature stumbling toward her. "I mean, we…Rattus and I have to go. So thanks for everything. Um, bye."

Grammy had not yet completed her transformation. The thing pretending to be her grandmother hadn't changed entirely into a rat—only her face. Just the whiskers, black eyes, and the horribly wide grin.

"Don't leave this place," said Grammy-rat as she hobbled toward the two visitors who were attempting to sneak out the front door. "I want you to stay with me, always and forever, dear." To entice her fearful guests to stay, she held out the decorative plate, stacked high with homemade peanut butter fudge, sliced into small squares.

Miz was close enough to see that there were *things* crawling in, around, and through the light brown fudge. An assortment of household pests. Centipedes, beetles, ticks, spiders, and many other multi-legged insects, all enjoying the special treats.

"Look!" Grammy continued to slink her way down the hallway carpet with awkward, jerky movements. Her aged body wasn't cooperating. "It's your favorite afterschool treat! Go on, sweetie, have a bite to eat. You and your little rat friend."

Miz needed something to distract her rat-faced Grammy, otherwise she might never get to the front door, let alone make it down the driveway, across the street, and over to the waiting train.

Just a few more steps to the front door…

"No thanks, Grammy." Miz did her best to not panic. But telling herself to *calm down* or *it'll be okay* simply made it worse. "I'm too full already." Thinking about the main ingredient in the peanut butter fudge was enough to turn her stomach.

"Don't run," Rattus whispered in her ear. "Just keep walking toward the door. That's it—*oops*!"

Rattus was frightened too. So worried, in fact, that he was unable to control his tiny bladder.

"Sorry."

Miz did as instructed. She ignored the wetness in her hand as she continued down the hallway to the front door, taking slow, careful steps. One stumble and Grammy-rat would be on top of her.

Out of the walls came more surprises.

An army of centipedes came crawling out of the cracks and gaps in the foyer walls. Then came all the others. Thousands of tiny black ants. Moths. Flies. Wasps.

Miz screamed again when a large family of sandy brown spiders with a little violin-shaped marking on their backs suddenly emerged. Some were as big as her hand, some bigger. All of them came rushing at her muddy feet, attempting to climb up her bare legs.

"Go on, dear. Try some fudge!" Grammy's voice was still her own, making the whisker-faced senior coming at her even more frightening.

"That's okay, Grammy," Miz said, her voice shaky and uneven. "I think I'd better go now. I have a, um…train to catch." Her heart was beating so hard that it made her head pound. She felt like she couldn't get enough air.

Beep-beep-beep.

A familiar noise filtered into her ears. It was the warning sound that her hearing aid batteries were getting low. Wandering around this horrible place, being chased by all of the monsters that her vivid imagination could come up with, while being unable to hear…was more than she could take.

"*Staaaay,*" croaked Grammy-rat.

Thinking she'd be safe once she reached the outside, Miz felt a new surge of fear wash over her when the thing that used to be her Grammy didn't stop pursuing them at the door. It stepped outside, turned left, and followed them down the driveway in its clumsy, twitchy steps, grinning the whole time, and offering the plate of infested treats.

"Watch out!" Rattus cried.

A child-sized rat wearing a princess dress and plastic tiara came speeding down the sidewalk in her hot pink Land Rover.

Squeak!

"Rattus, no!" Miz cried out to her small friend a split second before a road raging rat girl crashed into her legs at full speed.

Rattus leapt through the air and charged back toward the house. The little rat girl on four wheels made a sharp turn, then chased the speedy sewer dweller up the driveway.

"How about you, Mr. Rattus?" Grammy-rat bent down to hold the plate of goodies closer to the ground. "Would you like a tasty bite of—*Ack!*" The elderly rat woman let out a surprised cry when her granddaughter's furry, scabby, hungry little friend ignored the offered treats and instead ran right between her legs and out the other side. She didn't notice the speeding SUV until it was too late.

Crash.

The tray of peanut butter fudge went sailing into the air, then scattered across the driveway. Miss Avery, the delinquent rat girl, hurriedly scooped up one delicious square, gobbled it down in one bite, then grabbed another. After flipping the small black lever to reverse, she turned the electric vehicle around and chased the little helper rat across the lawn.

"Hurry!" Rattus said. "Get to the train!" He uttered a painful squeak when the toy car drove over his tail.

"Okay! Meet you there!" Miz shouted, then took off running so fast in her muddy socks that she tripped over her own feet. She stumbled to the ground, badly scraping her hands and knees.

Others joined in the fun too.

Down at the far end of the street were the scooter kids—or what used to be the scooter kids. Now they were kid-sized rats dressed in street clothes, pushing along on their two-wheeled racers, speeding down Skummelt Avenue to see what all the commotion was.

Squeeeak!

The rat boys circled around Miz, squealing and laughing as they smacked her with their long tails. All of them pushed around on their scooters with their thick, hairy legs. Some snapped their jaws and clicked their teeth, while others hissed or swiped at her with their sharp claws.

"Get away from me!" Miz swatted at the scooter rats with her boots, which were still in her hands instead of on her feet so she could run faster.

The passenger door on the train was still open. With a mischief of rats reaching out to grab her, clawing and scratching her skin, she was able to reach the platform steps, though not before one of the bigger scooter rats grabbed a fistful of her hair…then pulled.

One of her hearing aids came off. It was quickly stomped on, smashed to bits by the scooter rats.

Safely aboard the train, Miz quickly realized she wouldn't be safe for long. The great long locomotive parked in the middle of the road made no sound at all.

No whistle.

No rumbling engine.

And her friend was still in danger.

"Rattus, come on!" Miz cried from the bottom step. "Stop fooling around! Get in here!"

"I am not fooling around!" Rattus hollered as he first dashed one way, then the other. He was still trying to elude the giggling rat girl on the hot pink death trap.

"Get in here!"

"I am trying!" Rattus darted left and right, spun around a few times, then bolted for the passenger door with the little rat girl close behind. In a panic, he ran *under* the train instead of on the train.

Whoosh!

Miss Avery made another sharp turn and narrowly avoided a head-on collision with the train. Squealing with delight, she drove her toy car back to the sidewalk, in search of her next victim.

"Yoo-hoo!" said Grammy-rat, hardly ten yards from the train. She carried a plateful of rotted treats, bringing it to them with a wide grin on her hairy, misshapen face. Her large rat feet had broken through the fabric of her slip-ons. A row of fat pink toes wiggled from the ends of her mocha-colored orthopedic shoes.

Slam!

Rattus gave a sharp cry when Miz slammed the train door so fast that she nearly closed it on her friend's tail.

"Sorry!" Miz said. "Are you okay?"

Rattus panted heavily, but claimed he was unhurt. "Just lock the door! Before your Grammy gets here. Quick!"

"I can't lock it!" Miz shouted. "It's stuck!"

Grammy-rat walked right up to the door with the round window in the center. But she didn't stop once she'd reached it, or even go for the door handle. She just kept on walking until she plowed face-first into the cast-iron door, cracking the decorative plate in half, and spilling the specially made treats on the ground. But that was no deterrent for a grandmother with young mouths to feed.

With a few squares of "bug fudge" in each hand, Grammy-rat offered her frightened granddaughter a homemade snack while she continued to beat her head against the window, again and again.

"Fudge time, dear! It's your favorite!" said Grammy-rat as she attempted to use her head to break down the heavy door, grinning the whole time, showing off two rows of dull but powerful teeth.

Thump.

With all her might, Miz held the door shut as she desperately tried to keep *out* what desperately wanted *in*.

"Why isn't the train moving?" Miz shouted. "What's wrong with it? Shouldn't the engines be firing up? Or doing whatever engines do?"

From the top step, Rattus said, "I don't know why we're not moving. Maybe this is our last stop."

Each time Grammy-rat slammed her forehead into the window, Miz could feel the vibration travel up her arms. The glass was going to shatter any second now.

"Where are you going, *Miiiiz*?" asked Grammy-rat, continuing to bash her head into the small round window. "I made your favorite! PB squares with some extra tasty goodies!"

Thump.

"Grammy, stop!" Miz had to fight back tears as she struggled to keep the door closed. In her heart, she knew the thing outside was not her Grammy, but aside from the thick, wiry whiskers, it still looked and sounded just like her.

Rattus stood uselessly on the top step. He too was fascinated by the elderly rat attempting to use her thick skull to get inside the train.

"Don't just sit there! Help me!" Miz shouted. "Make the train move!" She let go with one hand to swat at him. To make him move, or do *something* to help, as if a sewer rat could somehow conduct a train.

"*You* make this train move," Rattus replied. "This is your imagination, remember? If you want this train to move, then make it move!"

Holding the door tight, Miz squeezed her eyes shut and imagined the train moving. Engines coming to life, pulling them far, far away from this awful place.

Thump.

Thump.

"Grammy, *please* stop…" Miz felt hot tears on her cheeks as the thing pretending to be her Grammy continued to gain access to the train by bashing her wrinkled face against the glass. Bruises had already formed on her cheeks, and a trail of red trickled from her nose.

Chuff, chuff, chuff.

An engine came to life! The dying locomotive had just enough left in it for one more trip.

"It's working!" Miz cheered when the train finally began to labor down the tracks, painfully slow, but still fast enough to escape a self-harming Grammy offering them a plate of bug-infested peanut butter fudge.

Ooooooo.

Whistle blowing, black cloud billowing from the smokestack, the train pulled away from Skummelt Avenue, rescuing them from the worst afterschool visit ever.

"What in the world took you so long?" Miz snapped at the rat seated across from her. "Those crazy rat boys on scooters were hitting me, biting me, and I still got to the train faster than you. And you have four legs!"

Rattus hissed in irritation. "Did you see the size of that girl chasing me? She was enormous! I'm going to see that little rat girl in my dreams!" He took a few raspy breaths, then coughed. "Being chased by that pigtailed rat girl probably knocked a month off my life!"

Miz was fuming mad at the whole situation. Too bad for Rattus, he just happened to be the only one in the vicinity to take out all that anger and frustration on. "I can't believe you did that! What were you thinking?"

"Me?" Rattus squeaked angrily. "I was trying to save your life! The world's worst three-year-old driver was about to plow into you, then that grotesque…*thing*…you call your Grammy would've been all over you."

Miz crossed her arms. "You almost got yourself killed!" she shouted, not sure why she was so upset. "Then what would happen to me? I'd be lost in this awful place, all alone, without anyone to help me." She turned to face the dirty window. She hated the fact she was so angry, and that she was being unfair to Rattus, which made her even more upset. Mostly she wanted to block out the disturbing image of Grammy's face knocking against the window— *thump, thump, thump*. And the awful grin, splitting her face in half. And those cold black eyes. And the stream of red that trickled from her nose, and down her wrinkled face.

Outside, the fog had returned. Nothing but shapes and shadows as far as the eye (human *or* rat) could see.

The train picked up speed as they continued down the tracks, bumping and rattling, while the only two passengers on board hardly spoke to each other.

CHAPTER 14

When Miz opened her eyes and allowed the strange surroundings to come into focus, the first thought to pop into her foggy mind was that she must still be dreaming. Traveling by passenger train as the world passed by the windows, just like being in some old movie. But if that was the case, it had to be the *lowest* low-budget movie ever made. The stale air gave off a moldy smell, seat springs dug into her skin, and across the booth lay a sleeping rat.

"Ohhh." Miz groaned when she sat up and stretched her stiff back. Not since she was little had she fallen asleep while sitting up. Passed out for only a short while, no more than an hour or two, it was a deep rest. Blissfully void of rats on scooters, rats driving toy cars, or an elderly rat with a wide grin and a plate full of fudge.

Rattus had also been lulled to sleep (again) by the constant shake, rattle, and roll of the train going down the bumpy tracks.

Miz had just set her mind to let him sleep a few more minutes before she woke him up to ask what they—what *she*—should do next. But the train gave a huge shudder that shook the entire car. Several curtain rods, a couple of tables, and junk from shelves and cupboards all crashed to the floor. It was such a bad jolt that Miz thought a wheel must've fallen off the train. She wondered how many miles they'd traveled. And how much longer the rickety old train would last.

"Hm? Where am I?" Rattus opened his black eyes and immediately grabbed for his left foot—the one missing a couple of toes. He also needed a moment to figure out where he was. Every day of his life he'd awoken in a foul, smelly sewer, so waking up on a train—even one as rundown as this one—was an improvement.

"Oh. Right. The train." Rattus slowly sat up and scratched himself all over, yawning and stretching.

Miz waited a moment before apologizing for the mean things she'd said to him after they'd made their narrow escape.

"I'm sorry about what I said earlier," she told the sleepy rat. "That was really mean of me. You really did try to stop me from getting hurt. So…thanks."

Rattus scratched his nose, his cheek, then several other spots before turning his furry head to the side, where he looked out the grimy window and away from the girl sitting across the booth. For the longest time he said nothing at all. Miz assumed he was still angry because she'd yelled at him.

"In stories, all those movies and books that people enjoy, it's the mice who are always cute and carrying swords," Rattus finally said. "But us? Rats? We're always portrayed as evil, awful, disease-carrying pests that only do bad things. Just the mere sight of a rat makes people extremely uncomfortable."

Miz had to agree, but kept silent.

"Mostly we rats wander around in search of enough food to survive," Rattus went on. "Rats live in the sewer—that's true. But where else do you expect unused imaginations to go?" For several miles he went on like this, defending his kind, not caring if anyone was listening to his rat tangent.

Miz tried to come up with one decent rat from a story she'd read, but was unimaginably stumped. She could have told him about Templeton, the rat from *Charlotte's Web*, but he was more comical than helpful. A fat, gluttonous, drunken rat. The only other story she could think of was *The Tale of Samuel Whiskers* by Beatrix Potter, where cute little Tom Kitten goes exploring, then almost ends up being eaten by two large rats.

"Okay, I get it," Miz interrupted. "But there have to be at least a few good rats in stories, right?" She immediately felt foolish for saying this because it was a flat out lie. People hate rats.

"Name one?" Rattus challenged her.

"What about Remy?" Miz suggested. "He was a nice rat who loved to cook. It's from the movie Ratatouille."

"Rat-a-who-y?"

Miz shook her head because she wasn't about to explain the entire premise of a Parisian rat who dreamed of becoming a chef.

"Never mind," she said. "I see your point. Most people don't like rats. But I'm glad you're here. You tried to save me from that awful, ugly thing pretending to be Grammy." She cringed from the vivid images that replayed in her mind. "You were very brave to do that."

"I…I was?" Rattus' small chest seemed to puff up. Then he had a terrible coughing fit that caused his furry chest to deflate, followed by a series of sneezes that brought on more red tears.

"You okay?" Miz asked when it was over.

"Sorry," Rattus said, wheezing. "It's this annoying respiratory infection. Don't worry, it's not contagious."

Mile after foggy mile, the train ambled down the tracks while its two passengers spoke occasionally, but mostly stared silently out the window. Rattus continued to sleep even as the noise of the train continued to grow worse as time went on. Somewhere up front in the unmanned engine compartment, the whistle blew angrily. The train itself seemed to be growing more and more hostile the longer it had to travel.

During the last stop, the clunky old passenger train barely got moving in time. And now with all the rumbling sounds, Miz thought there was a very good chance this would be the train's last trip.

Ooooooo.

With no watch on her wrist, no cell phone in her pocket, and no sunshine peeking through the clouds, it was impossible to tell (or even guess) the time. Although the weather outside was forever miserable, the gray clouds appeared just a little bit grayer. The dark sky seemed just a little bit darker.

Miz knew that at some point she would have to leave the train and find her way back home. Back to her family. Back to her brother, who was leaving for college and didn't have time for a younger sister. But right now, her mind was much too clogged with tough questions that had no simple answer. Why does everything have to change? Why do people have to change? Why are some imaginations lost?

Reiny, her ex-best friend (an idea that was still hard to accept) had certainly changed over the summer. Her brother had changed too, even though that started back when he was in middle school, then grew steadily worse over time. Her parents had changed by getting big promotions that led to more and more work. Extra work and less family time.

In barely a whisper, Miz uttered the words that had bothered her for a long time, and had now become so maddeningly apparent. "Why does *my* life have to change?"

No more than a few lengths of track had passed before she heard the reply of someone who'd lived and learned a lot during his 2 ½ years of life.

"Isn't life always about that?" Rattus said from his slumped position across the booth, eyes half open.

"What?"

"*Change*, of course."

Miz scrunched her eyebrows. "What do you mean?"

Rattus sat up and scratched himself. "Let's take you for example," he said, still a bit groggy. "A pretty young thing with clean hair, tasty-looking skin—"

"Okay, stop," Miz said, cutting him off. "My hair feels gross right now. It's crunchy and filthy. And practically my whole body is covered in mud and…other stuff." She cringed. "Just get on with your point, please."

The sewer rat showed surprising speed and agility

when he jumped down off the seat, scurried across the stained carpet, leapt over to her side of the booth in less than a two-count, then right up onto the seat and into her lap.

Miz hardly flinched. With the day she was having, it wasn't even a shock when her hand involuntarily lifted up off the cushion and gently stroked the rat's furry body—though she refused to touch his scabby tail again.

"My point is…" Rattus said as he nestled on her bare legs and gazed up at the girl with eyes as brown as the most delightful sewer tunnel. "One day your life is all about having fun and being creative. Drawing, painting, and making art, right?"

"Yeah. So?" Miz thought she was about to be attacked for her love of art. *Put away childish things*, and all that nonsense.

"And then one day you find yourself making eyes at some boy at school," Rattus went on. "Likewise with the girls, who laugh and giggle when unclever boys say foolish things."

Miz made a disgusted face to show just how truly revolted she was at the thought of liking boys more than art. The tight-lipped scowl and cocky tilt of her head made little impression on her small friend.

But the rat was right.

"Most of my friends—my *ex*-friends, I should say—are

already into that stuff," Miz admitted. "But not me."

While enjoying all the mindless petting and rubbing, Rattus rolled onto his side and briefly studied the girl with the dirty fingernails that were perfect for scratching fur mites.

"You never know, Mizzy Agnor," Rattus said, splayed out on his back. "You may change your mind one day."

"Not likely," Miz said, instantly rejecting the idea of ever liking a boy *more* than a friend. That rule even applied to Fenn, who loved making art as much as she did. "Boys smell. That's a fact. Have you ever been inside a gymnasium during PE class? Or had to ride home on a school bus full of stinky boys because your parents are too busy—or forgot—to pick you up?"

Rattus nibbled his itchy skin. "All I'm saying is that someday you might not mind so much."

The train was quiet for a mile or so—*inside*, but not outside. The high-pitched scream of the whistle sounded like it may explode from overuse. And the bumpy ride grew worse every second, making their voices tremble as they spoke. The passenger car they were seated in was vibrating so badly that soon it might be better to stand than to sit, or otherwise risk being tossed to the floor. The whole train sounded like it might fall apart if it didn't stop soon.

"Rats aren't typically attracted to one another by any particular smell," Rattus explained. "Mostly, we pee to attract a mate."

Miz jumped in her seat. "Don't you dare!" The rat in her lap went for a short flight. Luckily, he landed with a soft *plop* on the cushion next to her.

"I won't," Rattus said as he got himself situated. "I was just going to say that once, a long, long time ago—six months ago, at least—my life was going pretty well, if I do say so. I was rather well thought of within the sewer community. Many rats from all over the city came to me, seeking advice about which homes to invade, which office buildings to scavenge, and which dumpsters had the best finds…" He trailed off, reaching for his injured foot.

"Then what happened?" Miz asked. "Did the giant rat ruin everything? Did the Grundt attack you?"

Rattus shook his head. "No, it wasn't the Grundt," he said with an edge to his voice. A glazed over look appeared in his small black eyes. "A girl got involved. Isn't it always about a girl? Don't they *always* show up at the wrong time and spoil things?" He rolled onto his backside, held up his hind paw and wiggled the three remaining toes, as proof.

Miz felt the same bubble of fury in her stomach. The same one that turned to angry flames whenever some boy claimed they could do something better than a girl ever could, whether it was academics, sports, or just about anything.

"We don't spoil things," she said defensively. "Girls are

nice to each other. Unlike boys, who are always fighting, turning everything into a stupid competition, or saying mean things to each other."

Rattus laughed. "Always nice to each other, hmm?" He waited patiently for her to go on, keenly aware of how she was burying herself deeper.

"Yes, we are. Girls are just more——" Miz tried to think of the right word. "Oh, I don't know how to explain it. More mature, I guess. You wouldn't understand." She folded her arms across her chest, giving him a hard look that dared him to disagree, as if a sewer rat's life could possibly be more complicated than hers.

"Hey, it's okay. I get it," Rattus said, which sounded oddly familiar. "Sometimes a girl like you needs a little extra time for a thought to filter through."

Miz's mouth fell open. She had a cartoonish look of shock on her dirty face. Hearing those words thrown back at her felt like she'd just been sucker-punched in the stomach—or hit with a truth bomb.

Those were *her* words.

Spoken from the heart, just a few hours ago.

"That's not fair!" Miz protested. "I would never be mean to somebody on purpose. It just sort of——" She shrugged. "I don't know…came out like that."

The train was quiet (if only briefly) while the weight of this revelation sunk in. Sweet, kindhearted, mild-mannered

Mizzy Agnor had acted horribly to another person.

"I didn't mean to be cruel," Miz said quietly.

Rattus pulled on his whiskers. "Maybe not," he said. "But those words came from *your* mouth. Not mine. I heard them with my own ears! I was listening, remember? From the bottom of the ladder, back when this whole mess started."

Miz lowered her head, ashamed. With her eyes cast down on the train's ugly moquette carpet with its looping series of big and small circles, her mind flashed back to all the mean things she'd said to the people closest to her. She'd yelled at her brother—*twice*, just in the last two days. She'd also shouted at Fenn, her best friend, all because she was mad at someone else—her older brother, who was too busy to do anything with her, even though he was leaving for college. And she had even acted cold and mean toward Reiny, her ex-best friend. That was mostly because of Tracey Tispe, a girl with a cruel streak as long as a drainage pipe. The exact type of girl that Miz swore in her heart that she would never be like, no matter what.

"You're right," Miz said, dejected. "I did say those things. I guess I'm no better than her, am I? Stooping to her level, and all that stuff parents and teachers say, right? I acted exactly how I always swore that I would never, *ever* act. Just like a miserable, spoiled, pathetic—" She couldn't get her mouth to say the word…*bully*.

Rattus could tell he'd struck a nerve with the girl, since she looked about ready to cry. "Look at it this way," he said in a kinder voice. "Girls like Tracey Tispe often act out for one of two reasons. One reason is that their home life is very difficult. Lots of arguing, fighting, or lack of attention. And reason number two…"

Miz wiped her runny nose. "What?"

"Or someone else is tormenting *them*," Rattus told her. "And they are too ashamed to tell anyone. Too embarrassed to ask for help. Instead, they act horribly toward someone else to make themselves feel better. Usually it's someone smaller and weaker. Or perhaps someone quiet and shy, who prefers art brushes to sports and fashionable clothes and hanging out with boys. But it's the ones with true hatred inside them that have the real problem."

In her heart, Miz knew the rat was speaking the truth. Because it *hurt*. Lies could be stacked upon each other, built up like a house of cards, then topple easily and be quickly forgiven with a simple apology. But the truth, when it finally comes out, can have the crushing effect of a vice wrapped around your heart. It will squeeze, and squeeze, and *squeeeeze* until it feels like the poor wounded thing will break in two.

Miz broke down and cried, right there in front of the rat. Everything Rattus told her went around and around in her head, while the train rumbled down the tracks. The black treetops glided past the windows, never changing. She watched them go by for a long time. She was unsure what to do, what to think, and where to go.

Did anyone know she was missing? How long had she been gone? It felt like she'd been stuck on the train to nowhere for days, without food or water. The foul treat she ate at Grammy's house was like a brick in her guts. She was terribly thirsty, but her stomach turned at the thought of the "lemonade" from Grammy-rat's house. She cursed under her breath for not bringing along any supplies. A water bottle, tube of Chapstick, or even a pack of gum. All she'd brought was the windup flashlight. The one she'd dropped while climbing down the ladder and into—

The sewer.

"Hey, Rattus?"

The rat laying beside her was about to fall asleep again. His long tail was stretched out, with his back paws pulled close to his body, tucked in tight so no one would be tempted to use his remaining toes for a midnight snack.

"Rattus?"

"Hm?" Rattus sat up and rubbed his eyes. "What is it? Did you think up an idea for the next stop? Has that big imagination of yours finally dreamed up a way to get back home?"

Home.

That sounded nice.

"No. But I was thinking that maybe we should search the train," Miz suggested. "There could be some bottled water or something that might help us."

Rattus shook his head. "Don't waste your time," he told her through another yawn. "I looked already, remember? No food. No water. No *anything* on this train. Not even an engineer up front. The only thing I found was that tasty bit of fish a few cars down." His eyes darted all around, looking for it. "Speaking of which…where'd it go? That lovely, rotted fish head?"

Unable to stand the fishy smell any longer, Miz had snuck away from the booth while Rattus was dozing and tossed the nasty fish head into the black, moldy, bathroom of death in the next car.

"Besides," Rattus said, too lazy to get up and search for the spoiled piece of fish. "Don't you think it would be much wiser to figure out how to get back home?"

"Yes, I do." Miz pointed at the carpet, which had given her the idea in the first place. "That's exactly where I want to go. Back to where all this started."

The notion had come from staring at the worn out carpet with all the rips, moldy spots, and ugly stains. Mostly she'd been fixated on the twists, loops, and circles that made up the pattern. Each circle had a small dot, a starting point, then made its way back around again. Right back to the beginning.

"So? Where are we going? Are we off to—"

Eeeeeeeek!

Rocked by the sudden jolt of the train slamming on the brakes, the poor rat was knocked clear out of the booth. His tiny arms and legs kicked as he went sprawling through the air, then landed in a heap on the floor.

"Are you okay?" Miz had barely managed to stop herself from being knocked to the floor by holding on to the back of the seat. It nearly broke under the pressure, but kept her from slamming to the floor beside her small, dazed friend. She reached down to help him back up.

"Yes, I'm fine." Rattus took a moment to collect himself, then climbed into the girl's outstretched hand. He thanked her for the lift, then promptly climbed back into her warm lap to inquire about their next stop.

"You'll see in a second," Miz told him.

When the horrible squeal of brakes subsided and the train came to a full stop, Rattus squeaked with delight when he saw what was outside the window. Some of the fog had cleared away, at least enough to see the gaping hole with the murky brown water seeping out.

A short walk from the train was a tunnel wide enough that the men in orange vests could easily walk through, let alone a scrawny, artsy-fartsy middle schooler.

"Clever thinking," Rattus said, impressed. He missed his home too. "When in doubt—"

"Go back to the beginning," Miz finished.

With a rat perched on her shoulder, his scabby tail draped across the back of her neck, Miz left the train for the last time. She decided it was time to head back into the sewer, to confront her fears, and find her way home.

Somehow.

CHAPTER 15

Most sewer tunnels look (and smell) alike, so at first glance it appeared as if they'd been dumped off at the same entrance. Through the misty fog and light drizzle, even Miz realized the train had not dropped them off at the right place. The tunnel was still wide enough for her to walk upright, but also narrow enough that she could reach out her arms and touch the filthy bricks on either side.

"That's it, nice and easy," Rattus instructed. "Just keep walking in a straight line. Don't bump your head."

Miz was extremely grateful for the rubber boots on her feet, stolen from Grammy-rat's house. But if she didn't walk extremely slow and take care with each soggy step, the sludge of the sewer would spill over the tops of her boots. The foul water was almost a foot high.

Hardly a dozen steps in, the light from the opening of the tunnel grew dim. Just a few more steps and she'd lose what limited visibility there was, then be forced to rely on the rodent's eyes and keen senses.

"Where are we?" Miz asked the rat on her shoulder. "I mean, besides the sewer. I know that part. But the train didn't take us back to the right place. This doesn't look anything like the first tunnel we came down. It's a lot smaller. And there are way more pipes. And way more rats."

Chit-chit-chit.

Tens, hundreds, possibly even thousands of eyes— black, brown, pink—watched curiously as they walked past. Appearing to be an unfriendly group, none of the local rats made a move to attack. Most watched briefly from their tunnel, ledge, or vent, then went back to what they were doing.

A steady trickle of rats drifted down the tunnel on a piece of rotted wood, plastic water bottle, or some other piece of trash. Makeshift rafts created from toilet paper and disposable baby wipes, among other disgusting garbage. Some rats swam by with their tiny forepaws doing the dog paddle to keep their head above water. One or two rats even uttered a soft *squeak* as they went by, offering a quick hello to their fellow travelers of the underground.

Miz imagined that most of the rats were probably

wondering how on earth a girl had wandered so far from home, or traveled this deep into the labyrinth of the sewer. Perhaps they were also wondering why a rat, who *was* home, was traveling with the young girl, standing on her shoulder like a trained pet.

"Well?"

"I…I honestly don't know what to tell you," Rattus admitted. He tasted the air for scent molecules, using his ultra-sensitive nose to pick up on anything familiar, or dangerous. "I'm not sure where we are. I don't think I've ever been to this part of the sewer system. All these unfriendly-looking rats could be family for all I know."

Smaller cement tunnels veered off in countless other directions. There were also a ton of black, corrugated drainage pipes, which was where all the water (sludge) Miz was walking through kept pouring in from. Nearly every drainpipe had at least one rat peeking out. Many more were hiding in the shadows.

"Where do all those small black drains go?" Miz spoke mostly to calm her nerves. The circle of light behind them grew smaller with each step. "I wish they would stop leaking all this gross stuff I have to walk through. You're lucky to be up on my shoulder where you don't get splashed."

Rattus did his little sniffle-laugh right next to her ear. She felt his warm breath on her neck. "Those are residential sewer pipes," he explained. "They often serve as homes, or hiding spots, or for having a bit of fun."

"Fun?"

"Oh, sure!" Rattus said. "Rats are excellent swimmers. We can tread water for days! And we're good climbers too. A young rat can easily climb right up the drainpipes that lead to the bathroom."

A large family of rats watched them closely.

"Hey, I did it a few times myself when I was young," Rattus admitted. "Just for kicks. And *screams*, I suppose." He fondly recalled the days of his youth. "Ha! I'm so out of shape now that I might get stuck."

Miz cringed at the thought of sitting on the toilet while a rat snuck up the pipe behind her. That image would not be easily forgotten.

"What did you think happens after you flush?" Rattus laughed while the darkness grew thick around them. "It all comes down here with the rest of the wasted imaginations. To spoil, rot, and fester. To crumble, decay, and molder. To putrefy and—"

"Can we talk about something else, please?" Miz interrupted. "I don't want to think about this nasty stuff I'm walking through right now. The smell is bad enough."

Splash.

"Gross!" Miz tripped over something in the murky brown water and had to put a hand on the wall to stop herself from falling over. She wiped the foul mess on her favorite white shorts (that would be tossed in the trash, *if* she ever found her way out) and kept walking. The more she tried to *not* think of any place claustrophobic—closet, elevator, coffin—the more her imagination threatened to take her mind on a dangerous trip. Was the tunnel getting smaller? Was there less air to breathe? Would the tunnel overflow?

"By the way…" Rattus gently used one claw to push a long strand of the girl's filthy hair out of the way. "If you get any in your mouth…don't swallow."

"Thanks, Rattus." Miz would have laughed if she didn't so badly want to cry right now. She was pretty sure what he'd just suggested had happened at least once.

Splash.

Less than a few dozen steps into the tunnel, the light from the entrance was almost completely gone. The small dot of light she'd been relying on would soon be blotted out. Just like she'd imagined before, she was traveling down the length of a giant flashlight. Only this time she was moving in the wrong direction, *away* from the light.

"So…" Miz's steps were slow, but her heart was beating fast as she continued to take the rat's directions.

"So what?"

"If the Grundt is a boy's imagination—"

"A dead imagination," Rattus reminded her.

"Does that mean you were too? Did you once belong to someone creative?"

The air seemed to grow thick. Except for the dripping of raw sewage into the tunnel, the sewer had gone relatively quiet. Even the local rat population had scurried away, back up the drainpipes, off to their hiding spots and underground homes.

"Sorry, I didn't mean to be offensive," Miz said when no reply came. "I was just wondering."

"No, no. It's perfectly okay to ask such a personal question," Rattus said. "Yes, I was once the imagination of a child. The boy I used to belong to loved to build things. Lego towers that would fill his bedroom! Houses and cabins built of Lincoln Logs. Entire made-up worlds created with empty cereal boxes, milk cartons, and toilet paper rolls. Anything he could get his hands on, he would use to build."

This brought back fond memories for Miz too. Building a city of Lego with her brother, making a huge mess, and usually getting yelled at when Mom or Dad (usually Dad) stepped on a Lego brick they'd left on the floor.

"I honestly believed all his creativity—that is, *our* creativity—would lead him into architecture, design, or construction," Rattus went on. "But his older brother was having a rough time at school. And the only way he could think of to cope was to take it out on his sensitive younger brother, who once so greatly admired him."

"Oh. That's sad." Miz's heart broke for the boy's

imagination. She wanted to help all the abandoned imaginations down here in the sewer, lost and forgotten, left to die—or worse, clinging to the hope of being rescued one day. Reinserted back into the host child who gave them up one day, and who had most likely grown up to be another uncreative, unimaginative, unfulfilled adult.

Rattus breathed heavily in her ear. "I visited his house once—the boy, I mean. Dusty was his name. I climbed right up to his second-floor bedroom about this time last year, just to see what he was up to."

"You can climb that high?" Miz was impressed. Even though she didn't really want to know what went on in a boy's bedroom, she asked anyway. "Was the boy still making Lego cities? Building things? Being creative?"

Rattus shook his head. "Video games," he replied. "The boy I once belonged to was up on a school night at two a.m. He was playing some silly video game. I didn't see a single book in his room. Not that long ago, the boy used to have shelves filled with books."

Those words again—*used to*.

Miz nodded sadly. "Yeah, I keep thinking about those words a lot these days."

"What words?"

"Used to," Miz said. "Like how me and my brother *used to* draw all the time. Or how we *used to* have fun together. Like when we used to ride our bikes to the store and spend our allowance money on candy. Sometimes, if Dad let us borrow the car, he'd take me to Dairy Queen. Just the two of us. He always got an orange milkshake, and I always got a—"

"Shhh!"

Miz froze to the spot. The rat on her shoulder spun around several times, sniffing one way then the other, using his powerful senses to detect any sign of danger.

When Miz couldn't stand it any longer, she asked him what was going on. "What's wrong? Do you see—uh, smell something?"

Rattus' whole body was tense. He tried his best to not dig his claws into the girl's soft skin while attempting to locate the change in air molecules with the impeccable smell receptors inside his nose. "I can't smell any other rats. They've all run off somewhere. All I can smell now is…"

"What?" Miz asked. "I don't smell anything. Besides the stink of the sewer. Wait—"

Sniff.

"Popcorn," Rattus said. "I smell popcorn."

Miz was about to say that she could smell it too. Not the awful, burnt, vomit-like smell of microwave popcorn (the kind her older brother always stunk the house up with), but fresh buttery popcorn like they served at the movies. Before she got a word out, a loud ratcheting noise echoed down the tunnel. It sounded like…chattering teeth.

Chit-chit!

Catching a glimpse of even a small rat roaming around in broad daylight was bad enough. The mere sight of rats can instantly trigger feelings of anxiety.

"Oh, no," Rattus groaned.

When the unmistakable sound of a very *large* rat is coming toward you, its huge paws splashing in the water, grinding its teeth so loudly that the noise bounces off the walls of a dark, claustrophobic sewer…

"Quick! Hide!" Rattus squeaked. "It's him!"

"Who? The Grundt?"

"Yes!" Rattus squealed in her ear. His claws accidentally dug into her skin when he jumped from her shoulder to get away. He raced across a ledge toward a foot-wide cement pipe, then scurried down it and quickly disappeared from sight.

"Rattus, wait!" Miz had no time to run back to the entrance. The Grundt would catch her long before she made it to the end of the tunnel. The only thing left to do was take the rat's advice—hide.

Miz hid in the only side tunnel where she could fit. Half the size of the main tunnel, she was forced to kneel down, with the lower half of her body submerged in unimaginable filth. With her back pressed up against the wall, both hands clamped tightly over her mouth to suppress her rapid breathing, her eyes grew wide as the giant sewer dweller came into view.

CHIT-CHIT-CHIT!

When the Grundt finally appeared, it was a slow process because the rat was so big. An average sewer rat can grow to be anywhere from 16-20 inches from nose to tail. The "Viking" rat can reach a length of up to fifteen inches (not counting the tail).

The Grundt's body was twice the size of an adult capybara. An abnormally large creature that Miz had once observed at the zoo with her family, where she'd read the visitor info:

> *The capybara is the world's largest rodent. It can grow up to five feet in length and weigh as much as 150 pounds.*

The Grundt was a monster—a King Rat.

Sniff, sniff.

Its sensitive black nose twitched in the air, snorting and sniffing in all directions. It seemed to be having trouble locating the girl, when all it really had to do was turn its ugly head to the right, and it would easily spot her.

Waiting for the attack was the worst part. What would it feel like when those sharp claws shredded her soft skin? Or when those powerful jaws clamped down and she felt the gnawing, gnashing, grinding power of its four large incisors, able to chew through practically anything—

including lost girls.

Minutes passed.

The giant rat stood there for so long that Miz eventually got the impression that it really wasn't going to come after her at all. Was the gruesome rat doing this on purpose? Was it intentionally not moving in for the kill because it was enjoying itself? Hissing and coughing and making its presence known, the Grundt continued to make its obnoxious laughing sound, over and over, while she remained up to her waist in raw sewage.

Chit-chit-chit!

Chit-chit-chit!

When it appeared as though the Grundt had grown tired of tormenting the young girl, the monstrous rat moved on. Its huge body disappeared from view, creeping down the sewer in search of a more exciting victim.

Miz breathed a sigh of relief. But she was too nervous to find out if the giant rat was really gone, or if it was simply hiding around the corner. Instead, she crept farther into her grungy, foul-smelling hiding spot, where she would wait until Rattus informed her it was safe to come out.

Then came a flickering light.

And the unmistakable smell of popcorn.

"Wait a second—?" Miz's tiny, cramped hiding spot eventually opened up into an area much larger than any tunnel she'd had the displeasure of exploring so far. "There's an exit to this awful place?"

Hunched over, using both hands to feel her way down the tunnel, she inched her way toward the flickering light. She gently placed one foot in front of the other, trying to keep her boots from splashing in the brown water. Any extra noise could bring back the Grundt.

She felt instant relief (especially in her stiff back) when she was finally able to stand up straight. The small circular tunnel she'd been crouched in suddenly opened up into a wide open space. There wasn't enough light to see exactly where she was, but the familiar scent was much stronger here.

"I smell it too," Miz said quietly. "Popcorn."

Down a cement staircase, then along a short walkway, she passed a series of faded posters hanging on the crumbling walls. Each one was too water-stained to tell what they showed, but at least the floor was dry, so there was no more sewage to wade through.

When she pushed open the heavy door at the end of the hallway, she cautiously peeked inside and found the source of the flickering light.

"Hello?"

When no answer came, Miz entered the large room with its vaulted ceiling, patterned carpet, and heavy curtains draped along either side. Rows of cushioned chairs with red cloth and black armrests stretched across the entire room. And what she'd mistaken earlier for the

sound of chattering teeth was something else entirely.
was a rattling old movie projector, located high up on the
back wall.

A theater.

Only instead of entering from the back, she'd entered
from the front of the theater, right next to the screen. She
made her way up a slight incline, walking along the middle
aisle, taking careful steps in the darkened room.

"Hello?" Miz called again. "Is anyone here?"

Numbers flashed on the screen. The image was grainy,
but clear enough to see two large white circles split by two
black lines, separated with four gray squares. A timer hand
was counting backward, just like in the old black-and-
white movies.

8, 7, 6, 5, 4, 3, 2...

Miz took an aisle seat near the center row.
The show was about to begin.

CHAPTER 16

FADE IN:

EXTERIOR - STIGG MIDDLE SCHOOL - DAY

A normal day outside a two-story middle school. It's about 9 a.m. on a busy school morning. There are a few school buses in the parking lot. A trail of cars are driving away after making their drop-off. A crowd of kids and a few teachers are rushing up the steps toward the front door to beat the bell.

INTERIOR - STIGG MIDDLE SCHOOL - DAY

The inside of the school is busy and loud. Hundreds of kids are talking, goofing around, and searching their lockers for what they need for class (books, pens, etc.).

The school bell **RINGS**.

A clean cut middle school boy **EVAN AGNOR** is the last one left in the otherwise empty hallway. Already late for class, he is down on his knees and searching the very bottom of his locker to find the missing book - - his sketchbook.

SOUND F/X: DOOR CRASH.

Evan is startled by the loud noise.

Bursting from the stairwell next to his locker come three very large boys - - clearly football players, as each one is wearing their jersey. The smallest of these is **GRAHAM PIKK**, a greasy boy with a cheesy grin and narrow eyes. On the other side is **MICAH STORTAPER**, blond hair, piggish eyes, and a complete lack of emotion on his face. Last of all is **TERRY "THE GRUNDT"** as he is known throughout the school. Clearly the leader, he is big, strong, and wearing a cap to contain his wild, curly red hair.

THE GRUNDT
Check it out! It's the art nerd!

His obedient football friends laugh and surround their victim, blocking his escape. Evan is still on his knees.

THE GRUNDT (continuing)

You know you're late for class, right? Teacher might get mad at you. The principal might even call your mommy and tell them what a bad student you are.

More laughs from the GOONS.

EVAN (worried)

Yes, I know I'm late. You guys are late too. I'm just trying to find something so I can get to first period.

THE GRUNDT

Maybe I can help you find
what you're lookin' for, loser.

EVAN

I've got it, thanks.

When Evan tries to stand up, the two goons (GRAHAM and MICAH) hold him down on his knees.

EVAN

Can't you guys just leave me alone? Do we have to go through this every single day? Can't you find somebody else to annoy?

THE GRUNDT (oblivious)

Were you looking for this? Or maybe this?

How about this?

As the contents of Evan's locker spill out onto the floor, the goons laugh and cheer on their leader. Using his hands like two shovels, the Grundt doesn't stop until every last book, pen, and piece of paper is scattered across the hallway.

EVAN

Stop! You're making me even more late than

I already am! It's going to take me half of art

class to clean up this mess. Don't - -

Eyes wide with fear, Evan forgot that he'd placed his missing sketchbook at the very top of his locker - - out of sight for most kids, but easily within sight of a middle school football hero already well over six feet tall.

THE GRUNDT

Hey, what do we have here? Let's see what kind of

pictures the art nerd drew today. Look at all these cute

little drawings. Did you teach yourself to be an

artsy-fartsy loser, or were you born like that?

GOONS (in unison)

Born like that. Ha-ha-ha!

EVAN (upset)

Stop! Don't touch that!

SOUND F/X: PAPER RIPPING.

More laughs.

FADE OUT.

Miz wiped her eyes with the back of her hand. The scene lasted for less than two minutes, but she was already bawling. Seeing anyone being treated badly always made her feel sick to her stomach. But it hurt extra bad to watch her own brother being humiliated by a bunch of football goons. How could those boys be so cruel to someone so gentle and kind? So talented?

Tears rolled off her chin. There was no time to process what she'd just seen up on the screen because the next reel was already playing.

FADE IN:

INTERIOR - WOODWORKING CLASS - DAY

Sounds of lathes, drills, and chatter fill the shop. A class full of boys are working on their projects. The teacher is at the front with his feet kicked up on the desk and his face buried in a magazine (one that has nothing to do with woodworking).

Evan is on the lathe. He is carefully smoothing out a piece of wood he will use to make a birdhouse for his younger sister.

SOUND F/X: LOUD THUMP.

Evan loses his grip - - and nearly his hand - - when a heavy object slams him in the chest and knocks him backward. On the floor beside him is somebody's woodworking project - - a polished baseball carved from a piece of cedar.

THE GRUNDT
Strike! You're out!

With his arms raised in victory, the Grundt rejoins his laughing friends at the far table.

EXTERIOR - STIGG MIDDLE SCHOOL - LUNCH

The outside of the school is quiet. Lunch is in full swing. Most kids are inside the cafeteria, but a few scattered students are eating lunch in the shade of a tree or out on the field.

SOUND F/X: DOOR OPENS.

Evan is walking down a double set of stairs. He is reading a note that was delivered earlier - - in secret, by a girl.

SOUND F/X: SCUFFLING. SHOES ON CONCRETE.

The Grundt lands two solid punches before Evan realizes what's going on. His nose was buried in the girl's love letter, so he never saw the attacker hiding under the stairs.

GOON #1
Again! Hit him again, Big G!

GOON #2
Yeah! Mash his ugly face in!

Half a dozen football players are there watching. They'd been invited to watch the lunchtime sneak attack.

EVAN (confused)
What are you doing? What's your problem?

THE GRUNDT

You can have her. Enjoy, loser. Maybe she'll take care of

your boo-boos after I give you this...

Another punch. Then another. The Grundt is furious,
but Evan still doesn't know why. He has no idea it's because
of the letter he's holding - - from a girl who was the love
interest of the school's football star. When it becomes clear
that Evan isn't going to fight back, they all leave.

More laughs.

INTERIOR - STIGG MIDDLE SCHOOL - DAY

THE GRUNDT

Oops! Watch out!

Evan is violently shoved into his locker. A teacher sees the
whole thing, but does nothing - - keeps on walking.

INTERIOR - STIGG MIDDLE SCHOOL - DAY

In between classes, the hallway is busy and loud. Standing
at his locker with a couple of friends, talking and laughing,
Evan is grabbed from behind.

SOUND F/X: CLOTH TEARING.

The Grundt delivers a vicious wedgie that tears Evan's boxer shorts right off his body - - they are waved around in the air for everyone to see.

A ton of laughs.

Evan's friends try to help, but they are skinny, scrawny, artsy-fartsy kids like him. They too are shoved to the floor by the much larger squad of football goons.

THE GRUNDT
Stay down on the floor where you belong, losers.

GOONS
Yeah, losers! Ha-ha-ha!

Each goon takes a whack, kick, or swipe at the younger group of boys as they walk past. Evan has his hat stolen off his head. Nobody helps. When the show is over, everyone returns to what they were doing before.

FADE OUT.

Miz sobbed uncontrollably in her seat. Her nose was running so much that she was forced to use her arm as a napkin while the acts of violence continued to play up on the screen. The shaky black-and-white footage went on and on, with more unprovoked attacks, more hard shoves, more smacks in the back of the head, hallway trips, back-of-the-ear flicks, and even one sequence of what looked like half the football team (led by the Grundt) attempting to stuff her brother up and *into* a basketball hoop. Other students looked on, doing nothing to stop it, too worried about their own personal safety.

Miz wanted it to end. To just be over. But she couldn't manage to take her bleary eyes off the screen. Her brother had said nothing about any of this. Not to her, and not to their parents. If he had told someone what was going on at school, then she certainly would have heard some mention of it. Why didn't anyone help her brother?

In several scenes, a teacher was present in the background, either in the hallway or right there inside the classroom when the abuse was happening. But every time a teacher or grownup did intervene, it was either with a weak response to the situation, or merely telling the Grundt and his football friends to "knock it off" and then let them go without any punishment. Or worse, no response at all.

Flap-flap-flap-flap.

A noise at the back of the theater made her jump in

her seat. Scanning the large room, double-checking the rows of chairs, it was obvious she was the only one here.

"Hello?" Miz called out into the empty theater.

When the same noise happened again, the *flap-flap-flap* sound, it had clearly come from the projection booth. About to stand up to investigate, a shadow appeared at her feet. Then something brushed against her leg.

Miz screamed.

"There you are!" said a familiar voice. "I thought I'd find you in here."

"Oh, it's you," Miz said, relieved. She held a hand over her heart to calm herself. "Don't do that. You scared me."

Rattus climbed onto the seat next to her, where he remained expertly balanced on the back ledge of the chair, so he could watch the action on the screen.

"I went in search of the popcorn smell," Rattus told the girl. "I couldn't find any, so I went off in search of you. What are we watching?"

Miz sniffled. "It's a thousand and one scenes of someone I know being attacked and humiliated."

"Oh, I see," Rattus said. "That boy up on the screen looks oddly familiar. I've seen him before."

"It's my brother," Miz choked out.

Whoever was making all the noise up in the projection booth finally got the next reel playing. It was the worst one yet. The most painful to watch.

FADE IN:

INTERIOR - CLASSROOM - DAY

Drawings, paintings, and posters cover nearly every inch of wall. Shelves and cabinets are crammed with art supplies - - paint, brushes, clay, paper, pastels (etc.). Even the windows are covered in colorful designs and patterns. This is obviously the Art Room.

Evan sits at a long table inside the quiet, empty classroom. It's about 12 o'clock, lunchtime, so nobody else is around. He is hunched over his sketchbook and working feverishly on a new drawing. He is concentrating so hard that he doesn't notice three boys sneak into the room. It's the Grundt and his two most loyal goons (Graham and Micah).

SOUND F/X: DOOR SLAM.

This was only a decoy, so the Grundt could sneak up behind Evan and rip the sketchbook out of his hands. He roughly flips through the sketchbook while his two loyal goons surround Evan and keep him pinned to his seat.

THE GRUNDT

What's up, art nerd? Drawing another picture
for your mommy? Ooh, I like this one. Maybe
she'll hang it on the fridge for you.

Rips out a page and tosses it over his shoulder.

GOON #1

Ha-ha! Yeah. Fridge. Funny.

GOON #2

Good one, Big G.

EVAN (weakly)

Give it back.

THE GRUNDT

Nope. Sorry.

The Grundt tears out drawing after drawing from the
sketchbook and tosses them in the air, where they drift to the
ground. Each one is stomped on - - ruined.

EVAN (stronger)

Give it back! Now, you - -

The Grundt grabs Evan by the back of the neck and slams his face into the table. Evan is helpless - - and hurt.

THE GRUNDT

You what? What were you going to call me?

EVAN

Nothing.

THE GRUNDT

What'd you say, art nerd? Speak up! I can't hear you.

EVAN (weak)

Nothing.

THE GRUNDT

I can't hear you. What'd you say?

EVAN (weaker)

I said…nothing.

When there is no retaliation, the Grundt finally lets go. Evan sits up - - there is a trail of red streaming from his nose.

THE GRUNDT

That's right. You said nothing because you are nothing.
You're just a pathetic, artsy-fartsy nothing.

Evan is forced to watch as the Grundt tears the entire sketchbook apart - - every last drawing. When that's complete, the scattered drawings are further desecrated. Some drawings are crumpled up. Others torn in half. One goon rips a drawing with his teeth and spits it out.

Evan doesn't move. He stares at the table as this goes on around him. Because it's better than looking at all his hard work - - hundreds of hours worth of artwork - - being destroyed.

THE GRUNDT

Still drawing pictures? (Scoffs.) What a loser!

SOUND F/X: PAPER TEARING.

In the middle of the scene, something went wrong up in the projection booth. Either whoever was running the show hit the wrong button, or the film got stuck in the projector.

The scene kept repeating, over and over, until Miz finally had to shut her eyes and cover her ears to block it out.

THE GRUNDT

Still drawing pictures? (Scoffs.) What a loser!

SOUND F/X: PAPER TEARING.

THE GRUNDT

Still drawing pictures? (Scoffs.) What a loser!

SOUND F/X: PAPER TEARING.

THE GRUNDT

Still drawing pictures? (Scoffs.) What a loser!

Flap-flap-flap-flap-flap.
The projector had run out of film.

CHAPTER 17

Miz sank so far into her seat that she nearly slid out and dropped to the sticky floor in an attempt to get away from the images on the screen. She felt drained. Completely wiped out from learning the real reason why her brother decided to give up on his passion, his art, and bury his imagination so deep that it would never come out. Locked away where those painful memories would never hurt him again.

Miz wiped away the last of her tears. With nothing else handy, she blew her nose on her dirty shirt.

"At least now I know why he never wants to draw with me," Miz croaked out. Her voice was hoarse from crying so hard. "All this time I thought my brother just didn't want to be around me. Like art was a disease. Like I was a disease. I had no idea he had to go through—" She flicked a hand toward the screen. "All that crap."

Rattus was busy nibbling, biting, and scratching at the fur mites while still considering his thoughts about the film. He'd missed the first couple of scenes, but easily caught up with the basic plot that consisted of a group of football players crushing a boy's creative spirit.

"Using his imagination must've brought back all those painful memories," Rattus said. "Perhaps your brother thought that if he didn't use his imagination so much— or at all—then those bigger boys would finally leave him alone and give him some peace. Living at home with a creative person, such as yourself, must be as hard on him as it is on you."

Miz wiped a trail of snot with the back of her hand, not caring anymore about how terrible she must look.

"He should've told me," she said, struggling to sit up straight. Her back was hurting from sinking so far into the seat as she sobbed during the film, and her legs had pins-and-needles. "If he was too scared to fight back, then he should've told somebody. Mom, Dad—anybody. Why did he keep it a secret? Why didn't he tell me the truth about why he quit drawing when he was my age?"

Rattus had since jumped down from the seat in search of leftover junk food. Stale popcorn or a bit of old candy. He had to settle for licking the sweet, sticky spots on the floor.

Miz stared at the blank screen for a long time, not even thinking about anything in particular. Just sitting. Not moving, not figuring or planning, just trying to keep her mind blank. Anything was better than having those painful images of her brother being humiliated revolve inside her head—or worse, replay up on the screen.

"Well?" Rattus finally said.

"Well what?" Miz didn't feel like moving from her comfortable seat. Leaving the theater meant either going back the way she came (the sewer, and possibly right into the waiting claws of the Grundt) or stepping through the theater door and into some fresh new nightmare. Two perfectly good reasons to remain exactly where she was. A useless lump in a chair, inside an abandoned movie theater, lost somewhere in the underground.

Clunk.

All the strange noises, the clanging and banging coming from the projection booth, echoed down into the quiet theater. The noise would stop for a while, then start back up again.

A moment later, the same numbers were displayed up on the screen again, counting down. The awful memory-movie was about to start all over again.

"Why don't you go ask him?" Rattus flicked his nose toward the light shining out from the small window of the projection booth.

"Ask who?"

Rattus sniffed like he was annoyed. "Your brother, of course. The boy from the film we just watched is up there. I saw him earlier, when I went looking for some of that delicious-smelling popcorn—I mean, looking for *you*, of course."

Miz had no intention of sitting through the film *How My Brother Lost His Imagination* a second time. She was all cried out. Bones popping as she stood, she walked up the sloping aisle toward the exit, then pushed open the door.

Miz gasped. "This place is huge!" she said breathlessly. "This is the coolest—and *oldest*—movie theater I've ever seen."

"Ah, the delectable scent of popcorn!" Rattus said with his nose twitching. "I hope we find some soon. I'm starving."

When Miz pushed her way through the squeaky double door and got her first look of the lobby, she was surprised to find the abandoned movie theater was more glitter than gloom. Still terribly rundown, but in far better shape than she imagined it would be.

The checkered floor was dirty and discolored, but still sturdy enough to walk on, if she watched her step and avoided the holes and fallen debris.

Lots of windows and mirrors cast her reflection, though many were cracked and broken. The white marble walls were crumbling in a few areas, while some large sections had already fallen down. Still, the theater—at some point in the past—must have been packed with customers, enjoying a night out at a the movies.

"Look up there!" Miz pointed to the row of all-glass chandeliers hanging from the vaulted ceiling, where hundreds of teardrop-shaped rock crystals reflected the light. The ceiling itself was a great swooping arch, with an elaborate design of diamonds and squares.

"Let's hope that none of those fancy lights break loose," Rattus commented. "I'm afraid only one of us would survive that ordeal."

With that thought in mind, Miz quickened her pace and headed for the winding staircase leading up to the second floor, where a long balustrade stretched across the length of the theater.

Rattus trembled with excitement as they walked past the snack area. The smell of popcorn lingered in the stale air.

"Oh, rats." Rattus was upset because the counters, shelves, and industrial-sized popcorn makers were empty.

Miz coughed. "It's so dusty in here." She pulled her shirt up over her nose, but that only made her gag because her tank top smelled like the sewer.

"At least the lights still work," Rattus said, "so we don't have to walk around in the—"

Zzzt.

The lights went out.

"Rattus?" Miz stood in the dark, too nervous to move. She focused on controlling her breathing and *not* thinking about all the horrible things that could be hiding in the dark.

"I'm here, don't worry." Rattus tried to soothe the girl by reminding her that rats have excellent navigation skills even when it's pitch black. "Pick me up and I'll guide you through the—ah, never mind."

When the lights flickered and came back on, Miz let out a huge sigh of relief. "Thank goodness," she said as she placed her small friend up on her shoulder.

"Well, the lights work *occasionally*," Rattus said into her right ear, the one still with a hearing aid.

"Let's hope they stay on," Miz said as she made her way toward the stairs with the worn red carpet.

Up the winding staircase, careful not to step in any of the holes, she made it to the top without falling or twisting her ankle. Walking along the balcony, she did her best to avoid the debris—fallen lamps, broken glass, rotted wood, and a slew of dead rats—all the way to a narrow wooden door with a crooked sign.

EMPLOYEES ONLY
(Proj. Rm. 1)

Three rusty hinges that hadn't been opened in years were loud enough for the Grundt to hear all the way back in the sewer. The horrible squealing sound echoed throughout the entire lobby.

"Um—no way." Miz's chest tightened when she opened the door to reveal a dark, narrow stairwell. No handrail, no string attached to a light bulb, but plenty of dust and broken pieces of marble to slip on, and go tumbling down.

Rattus could sense the girl's hesitation. "This must be the right place," he said. "There's a light at the top."

Standing on her tiptoes, Miz could just barely make out a sliver of light coming from behind a closed door.

Miz climbed the stairwell one squeaky step at a time, worried that something behind the door at the top might jump out at her. With both arms outstretched, she carefully slid her hands up the wall for balance, while trying to watch her step. She had to rely on the rat's good senses to lead her, since the tiny bit of light at the top of the steps didn't help much.

"Well?" Rattus kept clicking his teeth as they slowly made their way toward the door—painted dark green, but appearing black. "It seems I was wrong."

"About what?" Miz was glad for the conversation. A welcome distraction from the spooky stairwell.

"It appears that not every unused or unwanted imagination turns into a rat," Rattus went on. "I now know that some escape. Or at least lock themselves away, where they can never be found."

Miz knocked gently on the door. Expecting to hear nothing from the other side, she was surprised when a gentle voice called out to her.

"Just a second!"

A moment later, the projection booth door opened. A boy around her age stood there. He had the same wavy brown hair drooping over his forehead, and the same chocolate brown eyes as her brother. He looked so much like the boy up on the screen, except his face was gaunt and dirty, and his clothes were shabby. He wore a tattered gray t-shirt that hung off his body, and ripped black jeans that he had to hold on to, otherwise they would fall off his narrow waist. But the boy had a warm, inviting smile.

Miz stood there, dumbfounded.

"Hi," said her younger-older brother.

"Um, hi." Miz couldn't help but feel a bit nervous despite this being her very own brother. The way he looked at her made it seem like he had no idea who was staring back at him.

The boy wasn't Evan *now*.

This was Evan *then*.

"It's me, Miz," she said. "I probably look awful, I know. That's because I've been wandering around a sewer all day."

The boy gave her a quizzical look. "Oh. Okay. It's good to meet you. I'm Evan."

Scratching softly on Miz's bare shoulder to get her attention, Rattus reminded the girl that it wasn't really her brother she was talking to. "He's just a stored memory that's been locked away," he whispered in her good ear. "He doesn't know who you are, or where you came from."

Miz nodded that she understood, though really, she didn't. This *was* her brother. Except that instead of being seven years apart, they were the same age.

"A talking rat?" Evan said. "What a great pet! Did you teach him how to talk? Can he do any tricks?"

Rattus gave an annoyed squeak.

"This is my friend Rattus," Miz told her younger-older brother. "I'd be completely lost without him. He helped me get through all the tunnels in the sewer."

"Sewer?" Evan looked confused. "Tunnels?"

"Uh, well—it's kind of a long story," Miz said with a shrug. "Never mind. I'll tell you about it some other time." She noticed how her younger-older brother peeked cautiously over her shoulder, then stepped back, retreating into his tiny hideaway.

The room itself was cramped and poorly lit, but still brighter and more welcoming than the creepy stairwell.

"Want to come in?" Evan asked excitedly. "Your pet rat can come too. I can show you how the projector works!

I haven't got to show anybody for a really long time." He paused. "Actually—*never*, I guess. You're the first person to come visit me."

Miz stepped through the door and was given a quick tour of the claustrophobic room. An old metal chair with no cushion was parked beside the bulky gray and black projector, which was taller than the operator himself. A sturdy wire rack was pushed up against one wall, loaded with rows of dented silver canisters. Hours and hours of more film.

On the far wall was an entire rack of old film reels dedicated to one name:

Hush, Rory

"Sorry, there's only one chair," Evan said. "But you can sit there if you like. I don't mind. Go ahead."

"That's okay," Miz said. "I can stand, it's fine."

Through the tiny cutout in the wall where the light from the projector shined through (the porthole), the same feature film was playing.

Taking up his usual seat beside the projector, Evan sat with his thin hands folded in his lap. He nervously tapped his bare feet on the floor, staring up at the pretty girl with stains and other stuff all over her clothes.

"So…you know how to run that thing?" Miz pointed to the huge machine that took up nearly half the room.

She guessed it had to be an antique, since most movies nowadays had gone digital. "It looks complicated."

"This? Nah, it's not complicated," Evan told her. "Wanna see how it works?" He looked so thrilled to give her a quick how-to lesson that she couldn't say no.

"Yeah, sure."

"Okay, so first I load the film into the supply reel," Evan explained, pointing to a sturdy metal rod. "Then I thread the film here, in between the lamp and the lens. That's how you can see the image up on the screen. The film also has to go around this part here, the sound drum, then make its snaky way up here, into the take-up reel." He checked the projector up and down, side to side, deciding if there was anything else important. "And that's about it."

The room went quiet.

"So, do you—" Miz knew what she wanted to say, but thought it might come off as rude, so chose her words carefully. "Do you spend a lot of time up here?"

Evan nodded enthusiastically. "Of course! I spend all my time in here. I don't ever go" —his eyes grew wide and fearful— "out there. Is that where you came from?" He seemed to shy away into his corner, as if trying to cloak himself in darkness, even pulling his feet up off the floor.

Miz studied her younger-older brother for a minute. She silently debated whether or not he was tricking her, just like he used to do. Judging by his fearful expression, and the way he drew his scrawny legs to his chest, she knew he had to be telling the truth. He really hadn't gone outside. Not ever. He stayed in here and watched movies of himself being abused and attacked and hurt, over and over and over again.

"Are you telling me that you've never left this room?" Miz asked. "Not even down those steps? To explore the theater?"

Evan shook his head, drawing his knees closer.

"The floor has holes you have to be careful to avoid," Miz went on, "but it's a pretty cool old theater. Lots of stuff to explore, if you watch your step when you leave."

Evan gasped. "Leave? Why would I ever want to leave? I live here. This is my home."

The door to the projection booth was still open. A terrifying mouth that was ready to swallow him up, then make him disappear into the darkness beyond.

"It's too bright out there," Evan said, trying to act brave in front of his two visitors. "I think I'd rather stay in here, where it's safe." He shivered. "I've never opened that door before. Honestly, I didn't even know that door *could* be opened. I just thought it was always locked."

"Come on, I'll help you—"

"NO!" Evan jumped off his chair so fast that it startled his guests. He started reading aloud the labels of the film cannisters, in hopes of enticing the girl with the rat to sit down and watch a movie with him, or at least change the subject to something less frightening.

Rattus whispered in her ear. "You've tried your best, Miz, but it's not going to work. I think we should leave now. If *you* found this place, and *I* found this place, then other rats can find it too. We need to go."

"I can't just leave him here," she whispered back. "He's my brother. My family. There has to be some way I can help. There's no way I'm going to let his imagination sit up here and rot along with everything else."

Evan's arms were loaded with film reels he thought his guests might enjoy if they simply sat down and watched with him, and stopped talking about scary things.

"When I saw you come into the theater, I played my favorites for you," Evan told her. "I've seen them so many times that I don't really know what they're about anymore. Were they any good? Did you like them?"

Miz tried her best to smile and nod, though she felt like crying again. To think that this miserable room was where her brother's imagination had gone, stored away years ago, buried so deep that those awful memories of the Grundt tormenting him at school every day could never hurt him again, stomping on his hopes of becoming an artist, making him give up on drawing, robbing his talent, stealing his dream…

She had an idea.

Trying hard not to spook him, Miz stepped forward and gently stroked his thin hair. It felt like fur.

"I've got a better idea," she told her younger-older brother. "There's something I want to show you."

She held out her hand.

"I—I can't," Evan said, pulling away. His back bumped up against the projector so hard that the film cannisters slipped from his grasp and went crashing to the floor. "I stay in here. In *this* place. I don't go out there. Not ever. I wouldn't know what to do out there. All alone. By myself."

Rattus sniffed the air. "We need to leave," he said with urgency. "We don't have much time."

Miz ignored him and focused on her younger-older brother, who she used to go to first (even before her parents) whenever she was scared, or had a nightmare, or when something bad happened at school.

"You're not going out there alone," Miz explained to the frightened memory of her brother, who was now cowering in the corner. She extended her dirty hand and told him, "I'm going with you."

When a hand like cold mist slipped into hers, and squeezed back, the darkness beyond the open projector booth door didn't seem so scary anymore.

CHAPTER
18

Standing at the end of the tunnel alongside her younger-older brother seemed eerily familiar. Miz was in the exact same position not too long ago. Sticking her face out into the fog, daring herself to step into the unknown while keeping her feet safely inside the sewer. She wondered what her younger-older brother might be thinking about as he stood at the edge.

"What's out there?" Evan extended one arm into the mist, then quickly pulled it back. "I've never even gone outside the projection booth before. I've been inside that room since—" A glossy look came over his eyes. He shrugged and said, "I don't really know how long I've been up there. Years, I guess."

Ooooooo.

When the train whistle blew, Evan jumped back so fast that Miz nearly lost her balance. The shock of having a living memory jump right through her was like taking a warm shower and suddenly turning the faucet to icy cold. She had goosebumps all over.

"What's that noise? Is it something dangerous? Is it going to get me?" Evan bolted for the door they'd all come through a moment ago. He yelled and pounded his fists against the thick metal.

"Evan, stop!" Miz pleaded. "You can't get back that way. That door weighs a million pounds!"

During the short walk to the tunnel exit, Miz hardly noticed the rusty metal door built right into the slimy brick wall.

"I wanna go back!" Evan yelled. "Take me back!"

When they'd all left the theater lobby and stepped into the sewer, the loud *clunk* as the door automatically shut behind them was a clear indicator that it was an exit only. No re-entry. The heavy door reminded Miz of a bank vault, with steel rods going up and down, side to side, meticulously sealed and impossible to break down.

Evan continued to fight his way back, growing more fearful by the second. Miz reached out and gently placed a hand on her brother's shoulder to stop him from running down the sewer in search of another way back to his lonely projection booth. Touching him was like plunging her hand into a storm cloud, cold and empty, but bristling with energy.

"It's just a train," she told her younger-older brother. "A train that will take you wherever you can dream up."

"An Imagination Train!" Rattus chimed in.

"Yeah, exactly." Miz offered her frightened brother the best smile she could. It wasn't a *complete* lie. She just didn't bother to mention how every place that she'd dreamt up had turned into a rat-infested nightmare that would probably stay with her forever.

Evan's shoulders slumped as he backed away from the door. "I don't have a choice, do I?"

Miz kept quiet as she watched her younger-older brother slink past her, head hanging low. His feet made no ripples or splashes in the murky brown water.

"So, I just…" Evan stuck one foot out into the fog, then did the same with the other. "Walk straight ahead? What if there's a cliff? Or a bear? Or a creepy haunted house with monsters inside?"

Miz shook her head. "I promise, there's nothing like that out there," she reassured him. "I'd go with you, but I have to get back. My parents must be worried sick about me." She lowered her head. "Maybe."

Rattus dug his claws into her shoulder, then whispered in her ear. "They *are*," he told her. "You know they are."

212

Miz's throat clenched as she fought back another wave of tears. She had to be tough not only for herself, but for the living memory standing ten feet away, staring at her with a septic tank full of fear behind his eyes.

"Can you come with me?" Evan pleaded. "We can go any place you like. I'll be good, I swear! I won't complain or anything, I promise. Please?"

Miz shivered at the thought of getting back on the train again. Images of rat faces and chattering teeth were still fresh in her mind.

"Not this time," she told him, choking up. "You have to go on your own. Otherwise we might go where *my* imagination dreams up. I want you to use *your* imagination."

Evan gave a pitiful nod. "But what if I can't think of anything? Or what if the place I dream up is awful? What if the people are awful? What if they laugh at me?"

Hands on her hips, a stern look on her dirty face, Miz looked this timid, uncertain version of her brother right in the eyes and practically shouted, "Then let them laugh!"

Her words echoed down the tunnel.

Miz knew they were spoken as much to her brother as to herself. "The only reason you quit drawing was because you allowed somebody else's opinion to take hold," she told him. "That's why you let it go. And the only way for you to get it back is to get on that train and find it."

Evan's face turned thoughtful, like he'd suddenly

remembered some important piece of information that had disappeared into the thick fog just a few feet from where he stood.

"Yeah, drawing," her brother said. "That does sound familiar. Did I used to…draw? Make art? Create pictures and design buildings and stuff like that?"

Miz nodded. "Yes, you used to be really good at all those things. And that's why you're going out there." She pointed outside. "To take back what you lost. To wake up the imagination you locked away all those years ago."

Somewhere out in the unknown, the familiar sound of the locomotive drifted into the tunnel. The train engine came to life, ready for one last ride.

Chuff, chuff, chuff.

"Hurry!" Miz told her brother. "Go now, before it's too late!"

The train was preparing to leave with or without any passengers. After a brief embrace that was like trying to hug a hologram, Miz waved goodbye as her younger-older brother took his first tentative steps. She cheered him on, wishing him luck as he disappeared into the fog.

"Bye, Evan!" Miz let the tears she'd been holding back roll down her cheeks. She imagined this was what it would be like to say goodbye when her brother—her *real* brother—left for college.

Rattus squeaked. "Good luck out there! I hope you

find what you're looking for!"

When the sound of the train rolling down the tracks was too faint for her one hearing aid to pick up anymore, Miz turned back to face the sewer. Now it was her turn to be brave.

"Rattus?" Miz turned her head slightly to the right, where a sewer rat was comfortably perched on her shoulder. She saw the rat's tiny mouth move, probably saying something like…*Don't worry, he'll be fine out there*. But her hearing aid battery was so low that she couldn't quite make out exactly what he'd said. "Can you show me the way out of the sewer? I think I'd like to go home now. Will you take me back to the beginning?"

"Of course," Rattus told her. "That way!" He pointed one claw down the long, dark tunnel. This was not the same tunnel as before, but he assured the girl (whether she heard or not) that he could use his extraordinary rat senses to find the way back.

Before she'd taken more than five steps down the tunnel, sensing the dark closing in all around her, she felt his tiny claws dig into her shoulder. Since her back was turned and her hearing aid battery was failing, the sound of the metal door clicking open, shutting, then clicking open again had gone unnoticed. The rat on her shoulder was desperately trying to get her attention.

"What are you saying?" Miz asked him, sensing his

urgency. It sounded like he was saying…*Done? Some?* "Rattus, speak up. Did you say *dumb*? Or *fun*?"

The heavy door leading from the movie theater into the sewer—the one that looked like a bank vault on this side, but was nothing but a simple push bar on the other side—was suddenly shoved open.

CHIT-CHIT-CHIT!

Miz's hearing aid battery was nearly dead. But after several attempts, she finally heard what Rattus was shouting in her ear—a single word.

"Run."

CHAPTER
19

The Grundt was much bigger (alarmingly bigger) than any other sewer dweller. Aggressive, determined, and with four powerful incisors each the size of a pack of cigarettes. Being such a large rat also made him surprisingly slow. Which was the only reason why Miz was able to get away as quickly as she did. Thanks to Rattus' keen nighttime senses, he was able to navigate expertly in the dark.

"Turn right here!" Rattus shouted.

"This one?" Miz adjusted her ear piece, shoving it into her ear as far as it would go. Not even that helped. And the constant *beep-beep-beep* that kept interrupting, reminding her to charge her battery, was making her even more anxious.

"Yes, *that* tunnel!" Rattus said for the third time. "Hurry up, he's right behind you! I don't like that look in his eyes. I think he wants to inflict a great deal of harm upon both of us!"

Miz did as instructed.

The process of escaping down a pitch black tunnel was slow and difficult. She slid her left hand along the rounded brick wall to give herself at least some kind of reference to where she was. She had to force herself to not think about what her fingers were gliding through. But at least it was something tangible (albeit disgusting) that she could touch, while her other hand was out in front of her, reaching into the darkness, feeling for anything she might crash into— like a dead end.

Miz knew she had to pick up her slow pace, but still didn't have the courage to flat-out run in complete darkness. Not even with a rat on her shoulder who could see, sense, and use his whiskers to navigate, could she make herself sprint down a tunnel of the blackest black imaginable. What if she tripped and fell? What would happen when she couldn't hear at all? Or take any more directions? What if the Grundt knew a shortcut?

Falling face-down in a foul sewer, or completely losing her ability to hear would be the least of her problems if she didn't keep moving. If she didn't keep going, or gave up and tried to hide somewhere in the dark, the Grundt would easily hunt her down, then…take a bite.

Rattus kept shouting directions at her while working hard to remain balanced on the girl's shoulder. Things went well for the first few turns. His commands were heard, then immediately followed. But soon the girl began to panic, taking wrong turns, one after the other.

"No, I said turn left!" Rattus shouted. "You need to go the other way! I have no idea where this tunnel goes!"

Some tunnels had less muck to wade through, while others had a steady stream of filthy water that rose up past her ankles, making for slow progress. Miz ignored the water (and other yech) that had flooded into her boots and squished between her toes. She was almost glad her hearing was so faint. That way, she could no longer make out the splashing footsteps of the Grundt chasing them through the labyrinth of the sewer, or hear the awful *chit-chit-chit* of its four long incisors clicking at the heels of her rubber boots.

When Miz came to a sudden stop, her rat friend frantically shouted at her to keep going. His tiny paws padded across the back of her neck, shouting into each ear, yelling at her to keep running. But she couldn't even make out the sound of her own heavy breathing, let alone the tiny voice of a rat.

"What are you doing?" Rattus squealed. "Why'd you stop? Keep going!" He dug his claws into her bare skin to get her to press on down the tunnel. "The Grundt could be right behind us!"

At any time during all this, Rattus could have easily slipped down one of the smaller tunnels, or charged up a drainpipe, all the way up to someone's toilet to give them a wet fright. Instead, he chose to stay with the girl, who needed more help than he could offer.

When the Grundt caught up to them, he wouldn't be able to save her. Leaving the artsy-fartsy girl behind would haunt him for the rest of his life—however short that turned out to be.

"Just give me a second," Miz panted, "to catch my breath. My lungs feel like they're going to explode."

"I think—" Rattus tested the air. "I think you lost him. I don't know how…especially with all those missed cues and wrong turns you took…but I think the Grundt is gone."

"What?" Miz said.

"I *said*…I think we lost him. He's gone!" Rattus shouted with his nose right up to the girl's hearing aid. "The Grundt is—"

Squeak-squeak!

A large red eye glowed in the dark.

Miz went rigid.

Rattus peed.

With the battery so low in her hearing aid, only some of the words came through, soft and barely audible. She couldn't be sure, but it sounded an awful lot like two rats having a heated conversation—a lover's quarrel. Miz only picked up bits and pieces of the conversation.

"Girlfriend…"

"…bag of spoiled candy…"

"…Halloween…"

"Glowing bracelet…"

Through the constant low battery warning that kept ringing in her ear—*beep-beep-beep*—she was able to make out at least the first two words of what her rat friend was trying to tell her.

"Follow Rata!" shouted Rattus. "She's going to lead us back to the beginning!"

"Okay!" Miz couldn't exactly follow the rat named Rata, who was clearly the tougher (and louder) of the two, but she could follow the glowing red bracelet coiled around the lady rat's tail.

Traipsing along in the dark with her boots slopping and slurping in the muck was bad enough. Trekking through a sludge-filled sewer while Rattus and his on-again, off-again girlfriend continually yelled, squeaked, and squealed at each other was, unfortunately, filtering through her dying hearing aid just fine.

Squeak, squeak.

SQUEEEEAK!

Somewhere along the way, Miz thought she heard Rattus grumble, "Hoo boy, is she ever mad this time."

After what felt like hours, tunnel after tunnel, turn after turn, even forced to crawl up, over, and along a few ledges, a familiar scene appeared in the dim light.

Stars shone above.

The nighttime sky filtered in through the open manhole cover. All those tiny dots high above gave off just enough light to settle her nerves, knowing that a few feet above were her family, her friends, and some much-needed fresh air.

"Thanks, Rata!" hollered Rattus.

With a few more disgruntled squeaks, plus a great deal of angry teeth chattering at her infuriating boyfriend, Rata the lady rat disappeared up a drainpipe, leaving the spent glow-in-the-dark bracelet behind.

More tiny lights appeared.

Not lights, Miz quickly realized—*eyes*.

Hundreds of tiny eyes reflected the pale light pouring in from the open manhole, guiding her on the final steps of her underground journey.

"They're not going to attack me, are they?" Miz took slow, meticulous steps, being extra careful not to step on any tails.

"It's all right," Rattus told her, sensing the girl's fear at being surrounded by hundreds—if not *thousands*—of sewer rats. "They won't hurt you. They're trying to help. They dislike the Grundt as much as I do."

Standing directly underneath the open manhole cover, Miz's dry throat seized up during her first attempt to scream for help.

"Hello!" she shouted weakly. "I'm down here!"

Pale red light filtered into the sewer, on and off, then swirling around again. Although not strong enough to see properly down in the dark, it provided just enough light to know that *somebody* must be up there. The circling pattern made her think of a search light, or even the flashing lights on top of a police car.

Have I been gone that long?

Are people searching for me?

"HELLO!" Miz griped her raw throat. Unable to yell much louder than her normal speaking voice, she tried a few more times, then stood in the dark and waited for help to arrive. The beeping sound in her hearing aid had finally died, leaving her without the benefit of any sound.

Miz shivered in the soundless dark.

Off to her right were the faint shapes of the metal poles and broken rungs. The busted up ladder was still laying in a heap, scattered among the trickle of raw sewage.

After ten minutes of standing there and calling for help, still no one had arrived. Feeling helpless at the bottom of a dark pit, she was about to ask Rattus what was the point of coming here if the ladder was still unusable, when more light shined down into the sewer.

Yellow light.

The beam of a flashlight.

"Miz!" a voice shouted. "I found you!"

It was Fenn.

"I'm down here!" Miz hollered up to him, not caring how much it hurt to talk. She was miserably dehydrated.

"Miz, you won't believe this!" Fenn laid down on the grass to get a better look. The flashlight's beam illuminated his missing friend's face as he peered down the open manhole cover. "The whole neighborhood is looking for you! The police are here and everything. Your parents and your brother have been freaking out all day! Most of the grownups are off searching the woods. They all think you were kidnapped or something. I stayed behind in case you showed up—and because of my, um, allergies. Reiny is searching for you too. She's the one who told me about that Tracey Tispe girl throwing my sketch into the sewer. I didn't think you were crazy enough about art to actually go into the sewer. Even Mr. Drittsekk is out here searching for you. He's been telling the cops some weird story about the forest coming alive and attacking kids…and how his ghost-son who disappeared a long time ago is some kind of stitched-up monster…all sorts of crazy stuff."

When his lips stopped moving, Miz shouted up to him, "Fenn, I can't hear you. My hearing aid battery died. Just go get help!"

224

"Uh—okay!" Fenn gave her a thumbs-up. He pointed to himself, and then used sign language to spell out the letters H-E-L-P.

Miz felt like crying, she was so relieved.

"Don't go anywhere!" Fenn shouted down into the darkness, where his best friend had been since early this morning. "I'll find some rope or something to pull you up. Oh—hey! Mr. Drittsekk! Over here!"

Help was on the way.

Rattus climbed off the girl's shoulder, down the length of her arm, and ended up in her hand, bruxing his teeth and boggling his eyes, happy that he'd assisted.

Miz didn't even mind being licked by a rat.

"Thanks for all your help," Miz told her small friend. "I would never have gotten out of the sewer if it wasn't for you." She scratched behind his crusty ears. "Well, I'm not out yet, but at least you got me here safely. Thanks."

Rattus said something she didn't hear, then coiled his tail around her wrist to show his affection.

"Is this it, then? Will I ever see you again?" Miz wanted her sewer days to be done forever. But a visit from her helpful guide wouldn't be so bad.

"Oh, I wouldn't say that," Rattus said, though he knew the girl couldn't hear him. "I might show up someday. Especially if there's a juicy rotten fish lying around!"

"Did you say...*fish*?" Miz wiggled her hearing aid, unsure if she'd heard something or not. Maybe static.

Sniff, sniff.

"Are you okay?" Miz felt the rat's tail tighten around her wrist. "Don't worry, I'm not going to drop you, if that's what you're worried about."

Rattus squealed as loudly as he could. There was no time to explain that a rat's fur can become so filthy, so covered in waste from the sewer that it's nearly impossible to detect the scent of other sewer dwellers.

Miz knew something had to be wrong when Rattus suddenly arched his back. His fur stood up on end. Then his claws dug painfully into her skin.

"Rattus, what's wrong?" Miz was mad at herself for not telling Fenn to drop the flashlight down to her so she could at least see better while waiting for a rescue—something she would definitely give him guff about later.

Rattus was transfixed by the pile of broken metal that used to make up a twelve-foot ladder, now laying in a heap of rubbish. The perfect place to hide during a game of hide-and-seek in the dark.

At last, Miz saw it too.

Slithering out from underneath the pile of broken metal was a long tail, thick as a baseball bat and twice as long. Attached to the tail was the body of an enormous sewer dweller, lying in wait.

Miz had guessed correctly.

The Grundt knew a shortcut.

226

CHAPTER 20

THUMP.

Two large forepaws slammed into Miz's chest so hard that she was sent reeling backward. Her tailbone hit the cement first, followed by her elbow, then the back of her head. She hit the ground with such force that her other hearing aid came flying off. The small earpiece bounced somewhere down the tunnel and out of sight.

Miz rolled onto her side, while tiny bulbs of light danced before her eyes. The whole sewer seemed to be spinning around. "I think I'm going to be sick," she croaked, thinking this was the perfect place to do it. She sat up and was immediately slammed to the sewer floor again. This time, claws tore at her skin. From the left side of her neck, all the way down to the end of her shoulder, was a long cut that would make for an excellent scar—a permanent reminder, if she survived the next five minutes.

"Leave the girl alone!" Rattus shook himself off and prepared to fight. He too had gone airborne. Limping on his broken left leg (the one missing two toes), he found the strength to half jump, half crawl up onto the large, furry back of the Grundt, where he bit, clawed, and did anything he could to protect his friend. His four small but strong incisors were able to pierce the giant rat's tough skin.

"You dreadful deviant! You good-for-nothing goon!" Rattus shouted in between bites, scratches, and swipes with his claws. "You wicked warthog! You sneak! You parasite! We're all sick of you tormenting us. And making our lives miserable."

Though not for lack of trying, the Grundt had a tough time dealing with the much smaller rat that was painfully digging its claws into his back. The colossal rat spun in circles, twisted its head around, and snapped its jaws at the very vocal rat who was attempting to stir up his fellow rodents, urging them to join together in an underground uprising—a rat riot.

"Hear me, fellow rats! Now is the time to stand up to this indecent intimidator! This great terror of the tunnels! This filthy fearmonger! Join me, if you dare! Let us finally bring an end to this shameful sewer dweller!"

From the dark corners and smelly drainpipes, many other rats watched the battle, though none dared to intervene, or join the rat revolution. Their curious eyes simply reflected the light pouring in from the open manhole. Which now consisted of not only the stars and pale moonlight, but also two yellow flashlight beams that danced in the darkness, searching everywhere for the missing girl.

"Yell for help!" Rattus cried. "Call to your friend!"

Squeak!

Rattus gave a sharp cry when the Grundt clamped its powerful jaws down on his tail. Unable to defend himself while hanging upside-down, he fought bravely by kicking his feet and swiping his claws until he gave one final *squeak*. A last appeal to all the other rats to stand up for themselves. Then his small body went limp when the giant rat violently shook him side to side.

"Leave him alone!" Miz cried, then let out a sharp cry of her own when her helpful rat guide was mercilessly launched at the brick wall, tossed like a piece of trash. Rattus' small body hit the wall with a sickening *splat*, then fell to the ground and lay still.

The Grundt gave a loud victory squeak.

Out of the dark came a long snout, large pink eyes, mop of curly hair, and a mouth full of chattering teeth.

CHIT-CHIT-CHIT!

"Miz!" a voice shouted. "Where'd you go? Come back where we can see you! Mr. Drittsekk has some rope! We're going to pull you up!"

Miz heard none of it. The flashlight beams were clearly visible just a short way down the tunnel, which meant her rescuers were only a dozen yards away. But she had to get past the Grundt to get there. And the huge rat was having too much fun toying with her.

THUMP.

The Grundt was pushing her farther into the sewer, deeper into the darkness, where no one would come to the rescue. Or even if they did, by then it would be too late.

THUMP.

Miz attempted to drag herself to her feet each time she was shoved to the ground. After the third (fourth? fifth?) round of being knocked down, receiving new injuries each time, a familiar sensation began to replace the dizziness and nausea. It was that same bubble of fury in her stomach. The one that turned to angry flames whenever someone teased one of her friends, or laughed at them, or tried to hurt them. Only this time *she* was under attack.

"Is that all you can do? Push and shove?" Miz shouted at the Grundt. "Then go ahead!"

The Grundt obliged by shoving her to the ground once more. Then again, and again. Falling down each time brought pain to some new area. Still, none of the bruises,

230

cuts, or scrapes hurt as much as when the huge rat seized her by the ankle, clamping down with one strong forepaw. Then it dragged her back toward the light, so the two above-grounders could watch the girl's final moments—by flashlight.

"No, girlie," said the Grundt. "I can do a lot more than push and shove. A great deal more."

CHIT-CHIT.

The Grundt squealed its ratty laugh. "I can leave scars on your body—with *these*." A hint of light gleamed off four non-retractable claws as he continued to drag her down the tunnel, enjoying the look of fear on the girl's pretty, bleeding face.

"I can leave you with something much more unpleasant. How about nightmares to plague your sleep? The worst kind of nightmares that will stay with you even during the daylight. Fear-filled visions that will haunt you for the rest of your miserable life. Visions of…me."

Miz couldn't tell if she was so frightened that her mind was making this up, or if her minimal hearing without the hearing aids was somehow able to pick up on the Grundt's wretched voice as it spoke to her.

"When you fall asleep at night…you'll see my face."

CHIT-CHIT-CHIT!

"When you have a bad day…you'll see my face."

CHIT-CHIT-CHIT!

"When you're fifteen years old, or twenty years old, or even fifty years old…you'll see my face."

Click.

Suddenly she saw its face.

And she laughed.

Somewhere in the dark, her hand came across what she thought was her hearing aid—the one that came off when she hit her head. But it wasn't the hard plastic of her behind-the-ear listening device that was gripped in her hand.

It was the windup flashlight.

Zuzz, zuzz, zuzz.

What started out as the tinniest of whispers, nothing more than the sound of a soft rumbling, soon grew so loud that Miz swore she could hear it too. It wasn't the sound of clicking teeth, or static, or hissing.

The rats were laughing.

Even though most sewer rats knew about—or had at least heard of—the Grundt, a rat of epic size, none of them could say with any certainty what the giant rat actually looked like. Like them, the Grundt preferred to cling to the dark, hiding within the absence of light.

Now that the surrounding legion of rats—well over 5,000 rodents—could finally see the Grundt's dopey pink eyes, long slender snout, and mop of curly hair atop its odd-shaped head…they couldn't stop laughing.

Tsst! Tsst! Tsst!

Hsst! Hsst! Hsst!

In his fury, the Grundt lashed out at her one last time. A vicious swipe that tore a deep gash down nearly the entire length of her left arm. The giant rat took off running and was quickly swallowed up by the surrounding darkness of the sewer, leaving the tunnel wide open for her to escape.

Miz stumbled toward the light.

"Tie the rope around you!" Fenn shouted. "Nice and tight. I don't want you to slip and fall." He smacked a hand to his forehead when he remembered his friend couldn't hear him. Instead, he made a few quick hand gestures around his waist, showing her what to do so they could pull her to safety.

Miz just wanted to close her eyes. To fall into a deep, dreamless sleep. The loss of vital fluids was making her woozy. But she managed to do as her friend suggested, and tie the rope clumsily around her waist. She didn't even know if she'd made any kind of decent knot, or if she would just slip right out and plunge back down into the depths.

"We've gotcha! You're doing great!" Fenn kept hollering. "Whatever you do...don't let go of the rope. And don't you ever scare me like this again! I thought you really were gone forever."

Joy like she'd never experienced before surged through

her tired, battered, bruised body as Fenn and Mr. Drittsekk worked hard to pull her up.

Then…*pain*.

Tremendous pain in her foot.

The Grundt had only backed off, not run away. Angry from being laughed at and humiliated, the colossal rat leapt into the air on its powerful legs.

"AHH!" Miz screamed. "Pull me up! Pull me up!"

Four incredibly strong rat teeth plunged into her left foot, easily tearing through the rubber boot like it was nothing but soggy toilet paper—and sank in, *deep*.

Miz frantically kicked and pulled and shook her leg until she was finally able to dislodge the giant rat from her foot. The boot fell too, along with two small, fleshy prizes still inside.

Two juicy toes.

CHAPTER 21

Two men wearing orange vests and hardhats were across the street from the two middle schoolers sitting on the curb. A brand-new sewer lid was being installed because the last one had been stolen in the middle of the night, then sold for scrap metal.

Miz watched them work for a while before going back to her sketchpad. Seated next to her on the curb was her best friend. Somebody who loved art as much as she did, but who was also being supremely annoying this morning because he kept looking down at her injured foot.

"Will you please stop staring?" Miz was busy touching up her drawing with a few colored pencils from her emergency First-Art kit she had stashed in the front pouch of her new school backpack. She'd spent the last fifteen minutes sketching out a sprawling field of wildflowers. Only the brightest colors were chosen to make the scene as vivid as she possibly could—the complete opposite of the dull grays and heavy blacks of her recent adventure in the sewer.

"I wasn't staring at your foot," Fenn lied.

"Yes you were," Miz said. "Knock it off and finish your sketch, will you? It's one of your best ones yet. We've only got a few more minutes before we have to start walking. The last thing we need is to be late for our first day of middle school."

"I know, I know," Fenn said. "It's just—"

"What?"

"I've never known anyone with two missing toes before," Fenn said, unable to take his eyes off the thick padding of gauze sticking out from the side of her new sports sandals.

Miz gave an exasperated sigh. If she wanted to talk about it anymore—which she didn't, not after spending most of Sunday at the doctor's office getting shots, antibiotics, and a long lecture about the life-long consequences of living with missing appendages—she would have told him that it was the long cut on her arm that hurt more than the missing toes. The red, scabbed-over wound itched terribly under her long-sleeved shirt—specially chosen from her

236

closet to (hopefully) avoid the onslaught of nosy questions the kids from Stigg Middle School were bound to ask. Especially when she rolled into class on a shiny black knee scooter with four all-terrain tires, hand brakes, and a rack to carry her stuff.

"I can't believe you actually went into a sewer just to rescue one of my drawings." Fenn was impressed that his best friend thought so highly of his art, even though she still hadn't told him the full story.

"Did it smell?" he asked.

Miz placed her colored pencils back into her little black pouch, then closed her sketchbook. "It's a sewer, Fenn. What do you think it smelled like?"

"Oh. Right," Fenn said. "Probably pretty gross."

Ka-thunk.

The men in orange vests were done installing the new manhole cover, so placed the long metal hook into the back of the truck, then got in. The young worker in the driver's seat looked their way and gave them a quick wave before taking off down the road, headed for their next job. Several other sewer lids had gone missing across the city, so those also needed to be replaced. Reports of sewer rats roaming the neighborhood had also dramatically increased over the last 48 hours.

Miz was busy staring at the same piece of paper she'd been reading, off and on, since she'd sat down.

"Are you okay?" Fenn asked, noticing the pained expression on his friend's face. "Does your foot hurt? I told you we don't have to walk to school on our first day. My parents offered to drive us, remember?"

"No, it's not that," Miz said, a bit choked up. "It's *this* I just can't believe." The letter in her hand was what had her on the verge of tears—happy tears. The neatly folded sheet of paper was delivered into her hands early yesterday afternoon by her older brother, right before he gave them all one last hug, then drove five hours to his new college.

"What is that, anyway?" Fenn pointed to the letter. "It must be important. You've read it at least ten times already. And we've only been sitting here for a few minutes."

"My brother gave it to me," Miz told him. "Before he left for college." The letter in her hand was a reminder that something good had come from her horrible experience. Proof that a bit of light had emerged from the small projection booth where an imagination had been locked away for so long.

Miz handed over the scanned copy, where underneath the welcome message from the chancellor were the names of all the required classes for her brother's freshman year of business school.

Business Management
Business Law

Marketing

Human Resources

Business Ethics

Financial Management

Intro to Accounting

Business Administration

At the bottom, highlighted in yellow so there was no mistake that something *had* changed:

Graphic Design 101

Fenn handed back the paper, nodding his approval. "Hey, it's a start, right? Maybe your brother will get his business degree and open an art studio downtown. And you could be the manager—CEO, or whatever it's called. I'll work for you, of course, but I expect a really good salary like…I dunno, half a million dollars."

Miz felt a proud smile stretch across her chapped lips. No matter how much water, or juice, or milk she drank, she still felt so dehydrated.

Fenn was staring again. Not at her bandaged left foot this time, but at her shiny black ride.

"So…can I ride your scooter again? *Pleeease?*"

Miz rolled her eyes. "Yes, you can ride it," she said with a smile. "Just don't break it. The doctor said I have to use that thing for the next ten days. Then I have to wear a cam walker—one of those heavy black boots. Then I probably will want a ride to school every day, since my parents both leave for work so early."

"Don't worry, I won't break it," Fenn said as he whirled around the middle of the street on her fancy new scooter. He spun around in circles for a while, tested out the brakes, the turning ability, then suddenly stopped.

"Uh-oh. Look."

Walking up the hill toward them was her ex-best friend, Reiny Greene, who'd decided at the beginning of summer that cool kids, cool clothes, and acting snobby was better than being friends with artsy-fartsy types.

"Hi," Reiny said, acting a bit shy.

"Hi," Miz said back.

Reiny kicked at a rock. "Are you okay?" she asked after a long, uncomfortable pause. "I mean, besides the, um… toes and everything."

Miz tried to keep her cool. "Yeah, I'm okay. My foot doesn't really hurt that much. I'm just kind of nervous about our first day of middle school. I hope the teachers are nice." She could never be mean to her ex-best friend, even though Reiny had acted horribly toward *her* since the beginning of summer vacation.

"Yeah, me too," Reiny admitted. "I've heard there's a lot more homework in middle school. Not really looking forward to that, you know?" She shrugged. "And who knows, maybe we'll all have some classes together. I've got my class schedule right here, so we can check them out to see what teachers we've got."

Fenn kept whizzing around on the knee walker, pretending like he wasn't listening in on their conversation. He and Reiny had always been close too, but stopped being friendly to one another just as soon as the drama started up. He especially disliked how Reiny and Tracey Tispe (mostly Tracey) had teased them about sketching, drawing, and making art all the time.

"I like your new short hair," Miz said when the conversation stalled. There was a weirdness between them now, but still an underlying bond from being friends for so long.

"Really?" Reiny ran her fingers through her new layered bob haircut. "My mom freaked out when I told her I wanted to chop my hair off, so my dad ended up taking me to get it cut. I'm still getting used to it."

Miz was surprised when Reiny sat down on the curb beside her. Just like all three of them *used to*. Sit and draw, wave at random cars driving by, talk about the strangest things, and laugh until their sides hurt. They still had a few more minutes before they needed to get moving.

"So…where's Tracey?" Miz finally asked. "Did you two get tired of each other?" She instantly regretted saying it, though couldn't help being curious. And judging by the look on his face, Fenn wanted to know too.

Reiny dropped her gaze. "She's probably at Mike Tulette's house," she said bitterly. "They're a couple now—you know, going out and all that stuff. I think she's getting a ride to school with his parents."

Miz and Fenn exchanged a curious look, though neither one of them said anything. Several cars passed by before anyone spoke again.

Reiny let out a sigh. "She just—" Her shoulders slumped, then she said, "Mike Tulette is a jerk."

Fenn quietly mumbled, "Yeah, I'll say."

"He wanted to do things that I didn't want to do," Reiny went on. "So now he's going out with Tracey." With a scoff, she added, "They can have each other—those two sickos."

The street was quiet for a while. It was obvious that something had happened at one of Mike Tulette's parties that she didn't want to talk about. And Miz wasn't about to push to find out. She didn't care. All she cared about was that they were on speaking terms again.

"Well? Come on, then." Miz reached for her friend's extended hand, standing up with a grimace. Her injured foot always sent a jolt up her leg every time she stood up after sitting for too long.

"Aw, man! Is it time for school already?" Fenn asked. "I wish we still had another month of summer vacation."

"Me too," Reiny said. "I hardly did anything I wanted

to do this summer. All I did was go to a bunch of lame parties and hang around with stupid boys all summer." To Fenn, she said, "No offense, Fenn. You're not stupid—most times."

Fenn laughed. "Thanks. I think—?" Then he reluctantly handed over the cool new knee walker.

Miz eased her left leg up onto the cushion, trying to get it to where it didn't hurt so much. "I'm not sure if I'll be able to keep up with you two," she admitted. "I'm good at art, not riding scooters. We'd better hurry, though, or else we really will be late for our first class."

As a reunited trio, they walked (and wheeled) past Mr. Drittsekk's freshly trimmed grass, where a shiny new lid was visible just underneath the low-lying tree branches. Even though a brand-new manhole cover had just been installed, it still didn't make things safe.

Rats are clever.

They can *always* find a way out.

On their way to school, it didn't take long for her two best friends to ask what they'd been dying to know. Besides the obvious injury (one missing "ring" toe, one missing "pinky" toe) were all kinds of cuts and bite marks on her neck, face, and just about everywhere else. They'd barely made it down the hill before the questions about her sewer adventure came filtering into her brand-new hearing aids, complete with external indicators for when the batteries were running low.

"What really happened down there?" Fenn asked.

"Yeah, was it scary?" Reiny asked. "Me and my parents searched the whole neighborhood for you. Not even the police thought you might have gone down into the sewer."

"I'll bet the smell was awful."

"Was it dark?"

"Were there rats down there?"

Despite the warm sun shining down on this bright Monday morning, Miz's whole body involuntarily shook as she pushed along on her knee walker. She was ready for a brand-new kind of adventure—at a new school, along with her old friends. No matter how many times they asked, she refused to open up about her time spent in the sewer.

It was still too soon to talk about it.

Too awful to relive.

Maybe one day she would tell them all about it. But not today. Not until the sound of chattering teeth stopped ringing in her new behind-the-ear hearing aids with the ultra-crisp audio inputs that can pick up the smallest noises...like the clicking of tiny teeth.

Chit-chit-chit!

TWO WEEKS LATER...

For the first few days after being pulled from the sewer, Miz slept peacefully, all night, without waking up once—unless it was to go to the bathroom. Perhaps it was because she was so busy at school, or being exhausted from all the extra homework, or even the change in weather that she was able to sleep so well.

August had turned to September, bringing with it a bit of rain and some cooler temperatures.

Most nights she stayed up late with her sketchbook balanced on her knees, nestled in her comfy bed, drawing until she could hardly keep her eyes open. When life had settled down enough that she could finally relax because she was in a good middle school groove...the nightmares came.

Rat-mares.

The dream that had her tossing and turning this time was, yet again, infested with rats. Sometimes the rat dreams were simply reliving her experiences down in the sewer, where rats on scooters, rats on bikes, and elderly rats chased her down. The worst nightmare so far had been the one where not just one Grammy-rat, but an entire group of grandparent-rats came for a visit, including Fenn's grandparents (all still living) and Reiny's grandparents (most still living). They all offered her foul treats, polluted water, and came at her for hugs and kisses, with their hairy snouts, wiry whiskers, and sharp teeth coming closer, and closer, and closer.

"AH!" Miz startled awake. As usual, she was covered in sweat and breathing fast, with her heart thumping like crazy in her chest.

"Just a dream," Miz told herself. "Not real." The glow-in-the-dark clock hanging on her wall told her in bright orange numbers that it was 3:33 a.m. She flicked on her table lamp, squinting her eyes in the warm light. She took a few small sips from the glass of water she always kept beside her bed. Even now, after all this time, she could never seem to satisfy her thirst.

Miz took a few deep breaths, then checked to make sure her arms weren't covered in fur.

Tonight's dream had been one of the worst ones yet. It was the first one where *she* was a rat. Biting, scratching, clawing, grinding her teeth, and snapping her powerful jaws at her friends, teachers, and family.

Zuzz-zuzz-zuzz.

With the blue windup flashlight cranked up, shining its dull yellow light, she leaned over the edge of her bed to check underneath.

"See? No rats." Miz slid the flashlight back underneath her pillow, where she kept it every night, then lay her head back down.

The house was quiet. Her parents were sleeping soundly down the hall…there were no giant rats in her room…and it was time to get some rest.

The curtain moved.

In the dark, Miz took one of her hearing aids from the charger on the night table and slipped it over her ear. What she heard—or *thought* she heard—was a soft clicking noise at her bedroom window. With one hearing aid cranked up to full volume, the sound was still so faint that she couldn't tell if it was real or imagined. But with both of her hearing devices on, she heard it just fine.

A *tap-tap-tap* on her second-floor window.

In just the short amount of time it took her to get out of bed, flip on the bedroom light, then cross the room and pull back the curtain, the creature at her open window had chewed a hole through the mesh screen and slipped inside the house.

A rat was perched on the windowsill.

"I'm impressed," Miz said as she knelt down to be face-to-face with the rat. "So you weren't lying, I see. You really can climb this high."

Rattus' black eyes gleamed in the moonlight.

"Told you I could!" the rat said proudly. "It just took me a while longer than usual. I've been on the mend these last couple of weeks. My head is still a bit fuzzy, but my broken leg healed just fine. See?" He wiggled the foot missing two toes. "All healed up! Good as new—or *almost* new. Still missing the toes, of course."

Miz was extremely glad to see her rodent friend again. During her sewer battle with the Grundt, then being pulled up and through the manhole, she never got a chance to see if her helpful rat guide was still breathing after bravely trying to protect her.

"Speaking of toes…" Rattus peered over the edge of the windowsill. "I see Rata was telling the truth. The Grundt really did take something important from you. Does it hurt?"

Miz wiggled her left foot. She was wearing the art-themed socks her mom bought her, with a design of watercolors, paintbrushes, scissors, and colored markers. Even though the pain had mostly subsided, she wore socks all the time because the wound was still healing (*and* because it was a bit gross to look at, or think about).

"Ah, two missing digits," Rattus said wistfully. "Just like me! Two foregone phalanges. Two absent appendages. Two evacuated extremities. Two diced-up, sliced-up—"

"Okay, enough," Miz said, smirking.

Squeak!

In the far corner of the yard, over by the boxwood bushes, the wimpy beam of her windup flashlight was just barely able to shine some light on Rattus' girlfriend, who was nibbling on a rotten fish carcass.

"Hi, Rata!" Miz called softly, then received another high-pitched squeak in return.

"She's the one who took care of me after our little *incident* in the sewer," Rattus said, referring to the time a giant rat had nearly killed him. "Well, you know what happened, since you were there." He nibbled at the fur mites crawling all over his skin. "Rata's over there feasting on that lovely rotten fish you left underneath the bushes for us."

SQUEAK!

"Okay, dear!" Rattus told his impatient lady rat. "Sorry, I have to leave. I'm glad you're feeling better. See you around, Mizzy Agnor!" He snuck through the hole in the mesh in the blink of an eye.

"Wait!" Miz hollered so loudly that she thought her parents might hear, then come rushing in to check on her. The house remained quiet, so she whispered, "You never finished the story!"

Rattus paused on the ledge. Climbing up was hard enough. Getting back down would be that much harder.

"Whatever happened to the Grundt?" Miz asked through the screen. "Not the rat. I mean the boy who played football and won all those trophies."

Rattus came back to the window, much to the annoyance of his on-again, off-again girlfriend, who hadn't left him one bite of rotten fish.

"Last I heard, the football star went off to college about a year ago," he told her. "Some college about a five hour drive from here. Business degree."

Miz's eyes widened. "College?"

Rattus gazed up at her with his wet, black eyes. "Don't worry about your older brother," he told her. "He'll do just fine out in the world. Just worry about taking care of yourself, okay? Middle school may be tough, and you may have your own Grundt to deal with someday, but you have a big heart and a strong mind. It'll take courage, but—"

"What?" Miz asked, stifling a yawn.

"Well, I…" Rattus gave a thoughtful scratch. "I was going to say that after our little adventure in the sewer, I'm sure you can handle anything."

With a final parting *squeak*, Rattus was gone.

Miz pushed her forehead up to the mesh screen, where she was just barely able to watch her rat friend climb back down the clinging vines, claw his way across the trellis, then disappear into the night.

Miz closed the window, switched off the light, then slipped back into bed. Now that she was fully awake, she thought that perhaps drawing for a while might calm her brain down and make her sleepy.

A tremendous yawn had her pulling off her hearing aids and placing them back on the charger, where they would stay fully charged from here on out. With a soft *click*, she turned off the lamp, pulled the covers tight, then drifted off into a deep, rat-less sleep.

Art could wait until tomorrow.

Tonight was a school night.

INAUDIBLE

Thank you for reading Book 1 of the Quiet Man series. I hope you enjoyed this creepy adventure with Miz, Fenn, Reiny and Rattus, and that your imagination is still intact.

If you have time to leave a review, I would appreciate it! If you are brave enough, check out book 2, *Unspeakable*.

Follow the Author

Sign up for my newsletter to receive all the latest books and news at:

WWW.TEVINHANSEN.COM

Made in the USA
Middletown, DE
10 March 2023

26521774R00151